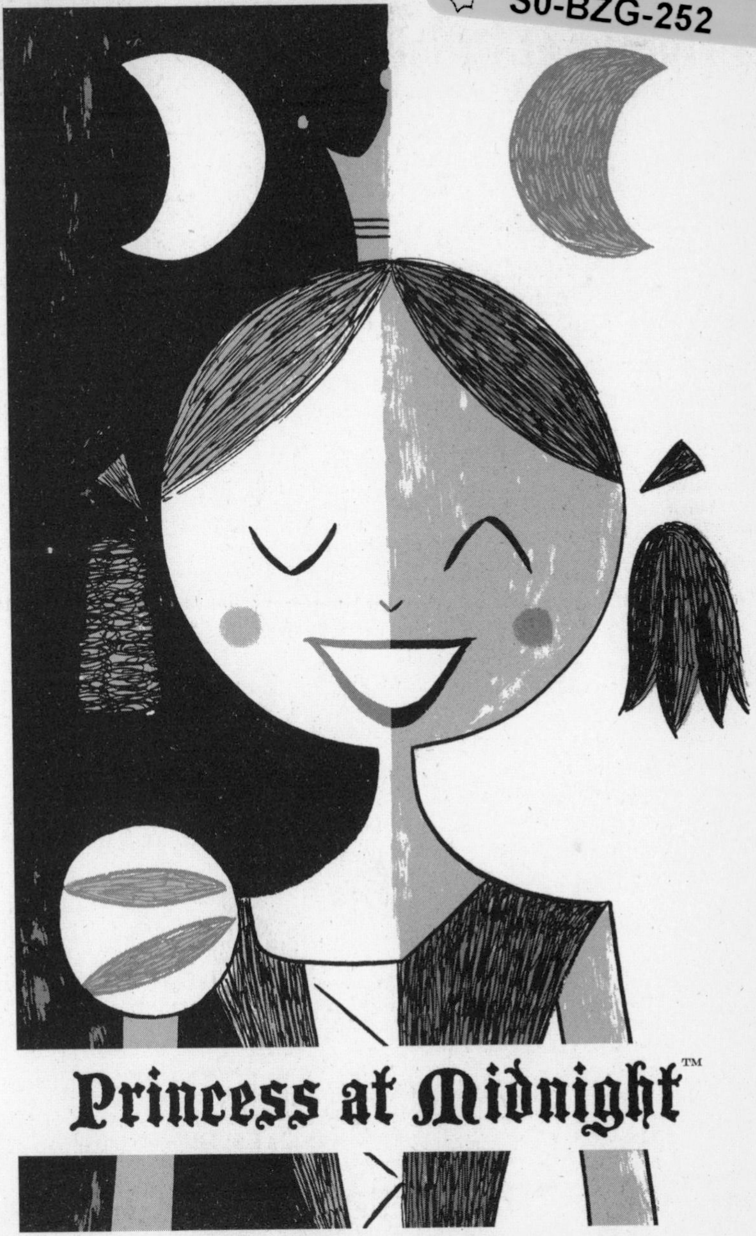

Princess at Midnight™

Princess at Midnight™

by Andi Watson

Thanks to Jamie S. Rich for
proofreading and trouble shooting.

**IMAGE
COMICS,
INC.**

Erik Larsen - *Publisher*
Todd McFarlane - *President*
Marc Silvestri - *CEO*
Jim Valentino - *Vice-President*

Eric Stephenson - *Executive Director*
Joe Keatinge - *PR & Marketing Coordinator*
Branwyn Bigglestone - *Accounts Manager*
Traci Hui - *Traffic Manager*
Allen Hui - *Production Manager*
Jonathan Chan - *Production Artist*
Drew Gill - *Production Artist*

www.imagecomics.com

PRINCESS AT MIDNIGHT
ISBN: 978-1-58240-925-2
First Printing

PRINTED IN CANADA

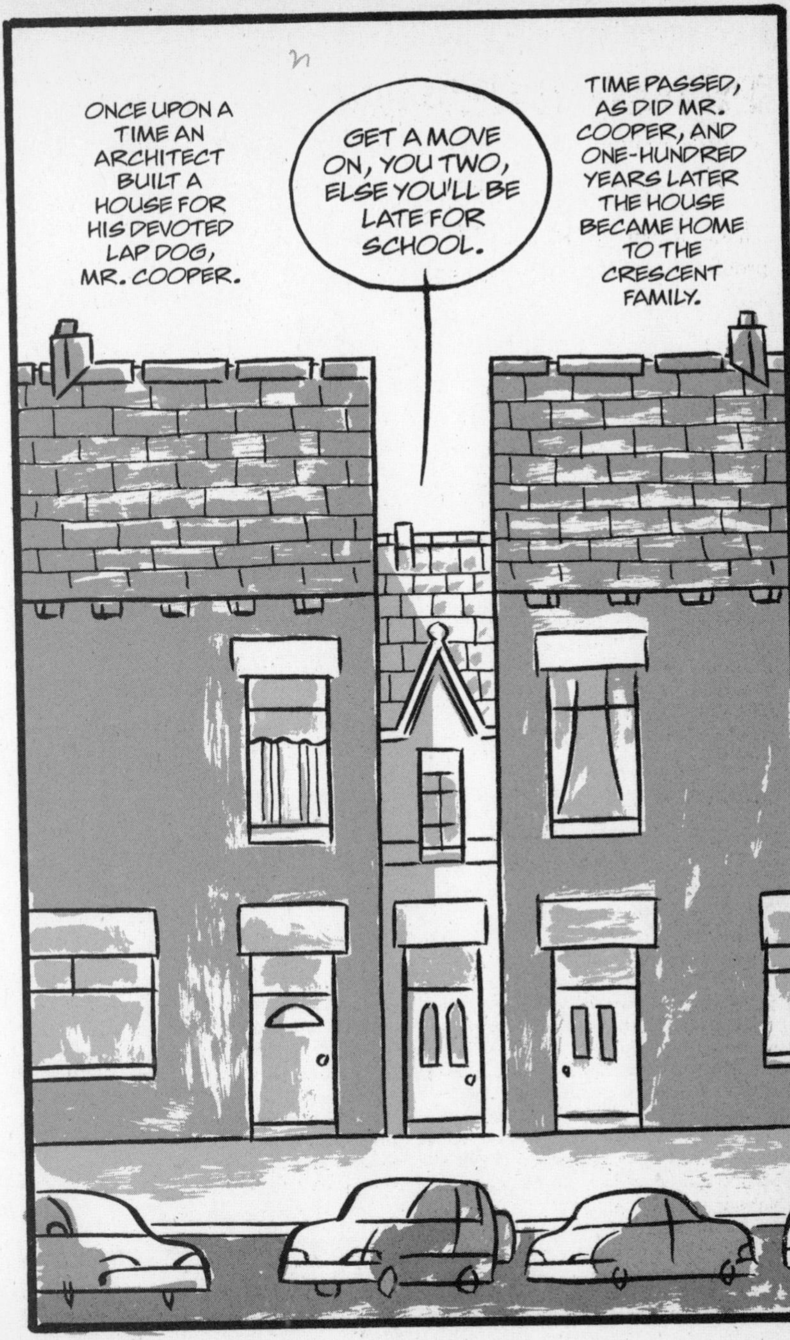
ONCE UPON A TIME AN ARCHITECT BUILT A HOUSE FOR HIS DEVOTED LAP DOG, MR. COOPER.
GET A MOVE ON, YOU TWO, ELSE YOU'LL BE LATE FOR SCHOOL.
TIME PASSED, AS DID MR. COOPER, AND ONE-HUNDRED YEARS LATER THE HOUSE BECAME HOME TO THE CRESCENT FAMILY.

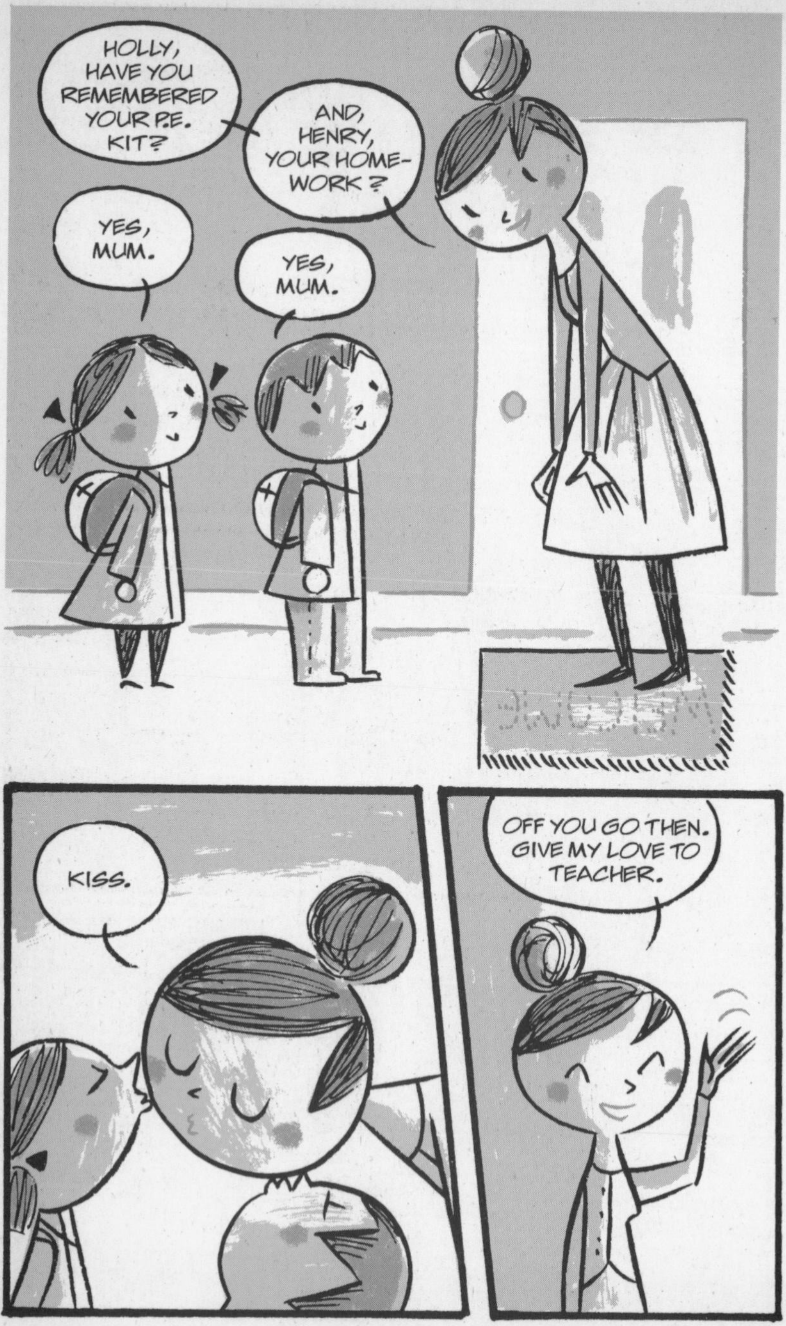
HOLLY, HAVE YOU REMEMBERED YOUR P.E. KIT?
AND, HENRY, YOUR HOME-WORK?
YES, MUM.
YES, MUM.
KISS.
OFF YOU GO THEN. GIVE MY LOVE TO TEACHER.

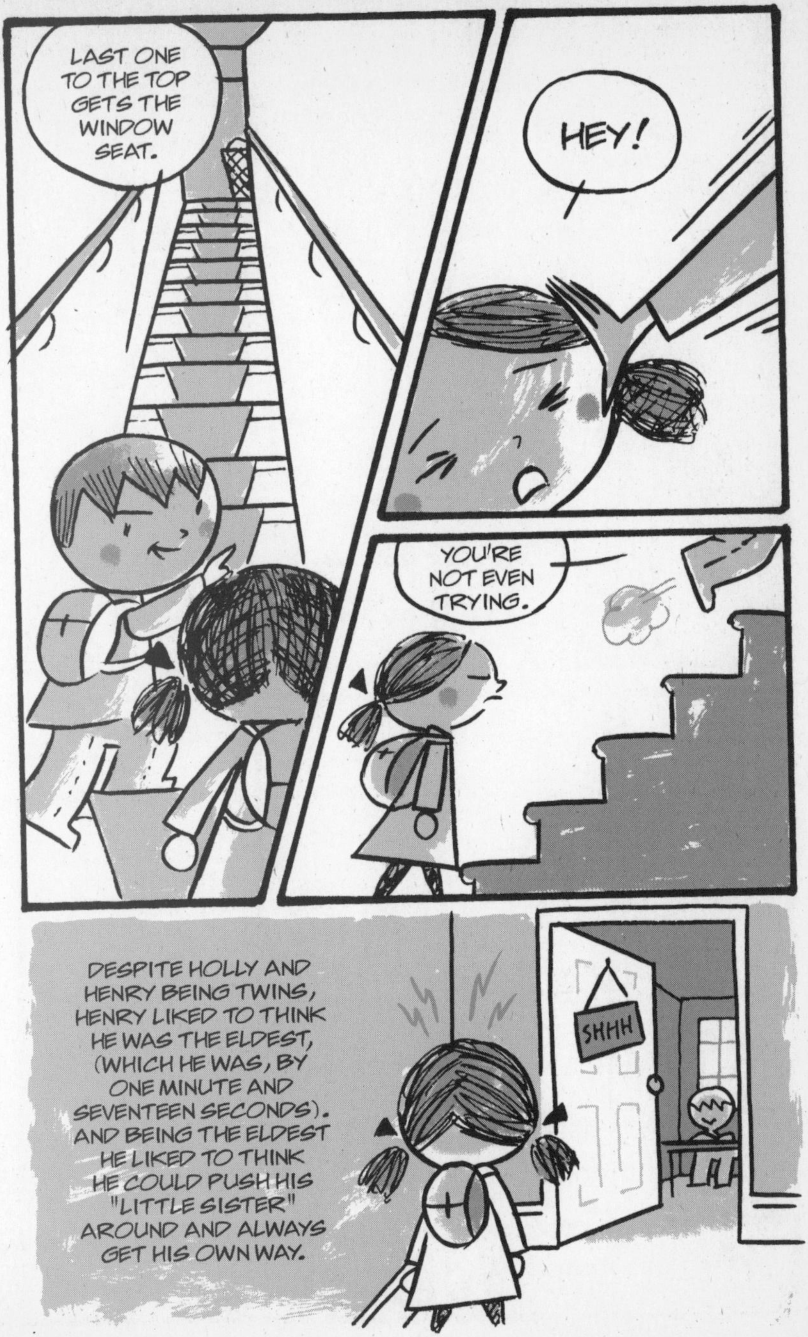
LAST ONE TO THE TOP GETS THE WINDOW SEAT.
HEY!
YOU'RE NOT EVEN TRYING.
DESPITE HOLLY AND HENRY BEING TWINS, HENRY LIKED TO THINK HE WAS THE ELDEST, (WHICH HE WAS, BY ONE MINUTE AND SEVENTEEN SECONDS). AND BEING THE ELDEST HE LIKED TO THINK HE COULD PUSH HIS "LITTLE SISTER" AROUND AND ALWAYS GET HIS OWN WAY.
SHHH

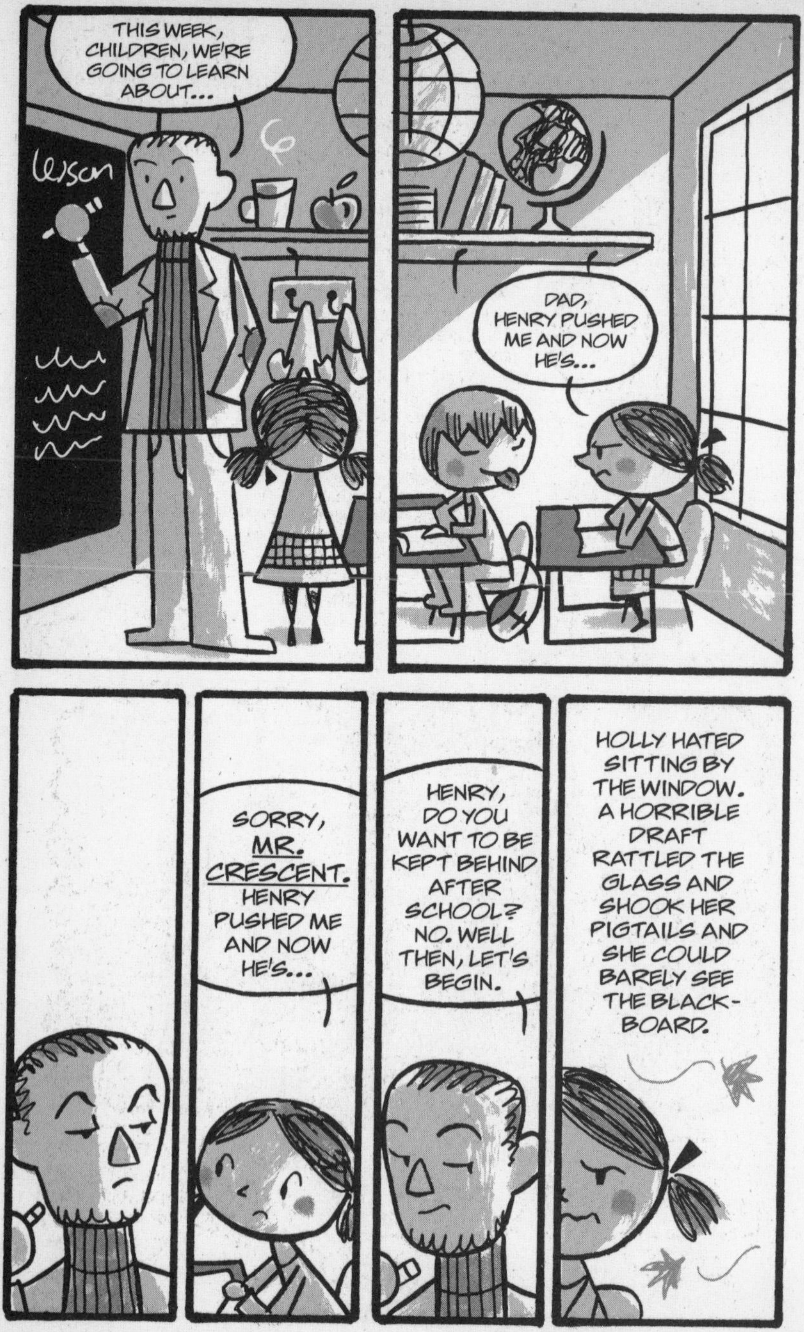

THIS WEEK, CHILDREN, WE'RE GOING TO LEARN ABOUT...
Lesson
DAD, HENRY PUSHED ME AND NOW HE'S...
SORRY, MR. CRESCENT. HENRY PUSHED ME AND NOW HE'S...
HENRY, DO YOU WANT TO BE KEPT BEHIND AFTER SCHOOL? NO. WELL THEN, LET'S BEGIN.
HOLLY HATED SITTING BY THE WINDOW. A HORRIBLE DRAFT RATTLED THE GLASS AND SHOOK HER PIGTAILS AND SHE COULD BARELY SEE THE BLACK-BOARD.

AHEM, AS I WAS SAYING, TODAY WE'RE GOING TO LEARN ABOUT THE COMMON AGRICULTURAL POLICY.

HOLLY'S DAD WAS PASSIONATE ABOUT HOME SCHOOLING BUT WAS ALSO PASSIONATE THAT IT SHOULD BE *EXACTLY* LIKE SCHOOL. EXCEPT FOR THE BITS THAT INCLUDED LAUGHING AND RUNNING AROUND AND HAVING FUN AND POSSIBLY FALLING AND GRAZING YOUR KNEES OR MEETING CHILDREN WHO WERE BIGGER THAN YOU AND MIGHT CALL YOU NAMES OR PUSH YOU OVER OR MAKE YOU CRY.

N REFERR AS THE *CAP*, IT TEM OF SUBSID TALLING FORTY R PERCENT O XPENDITU

HOLLY COULD HEAR THE BELL RING FOR PLAYTIME AT THE SCHOOL BEHIND HER HOUSE.

AST YEA THE TOTAL AME TO FORT NINE BILLION EUROS

HE AIM IS INSTITUTE MINIMUM PRI R PRODUC D BY PAYN

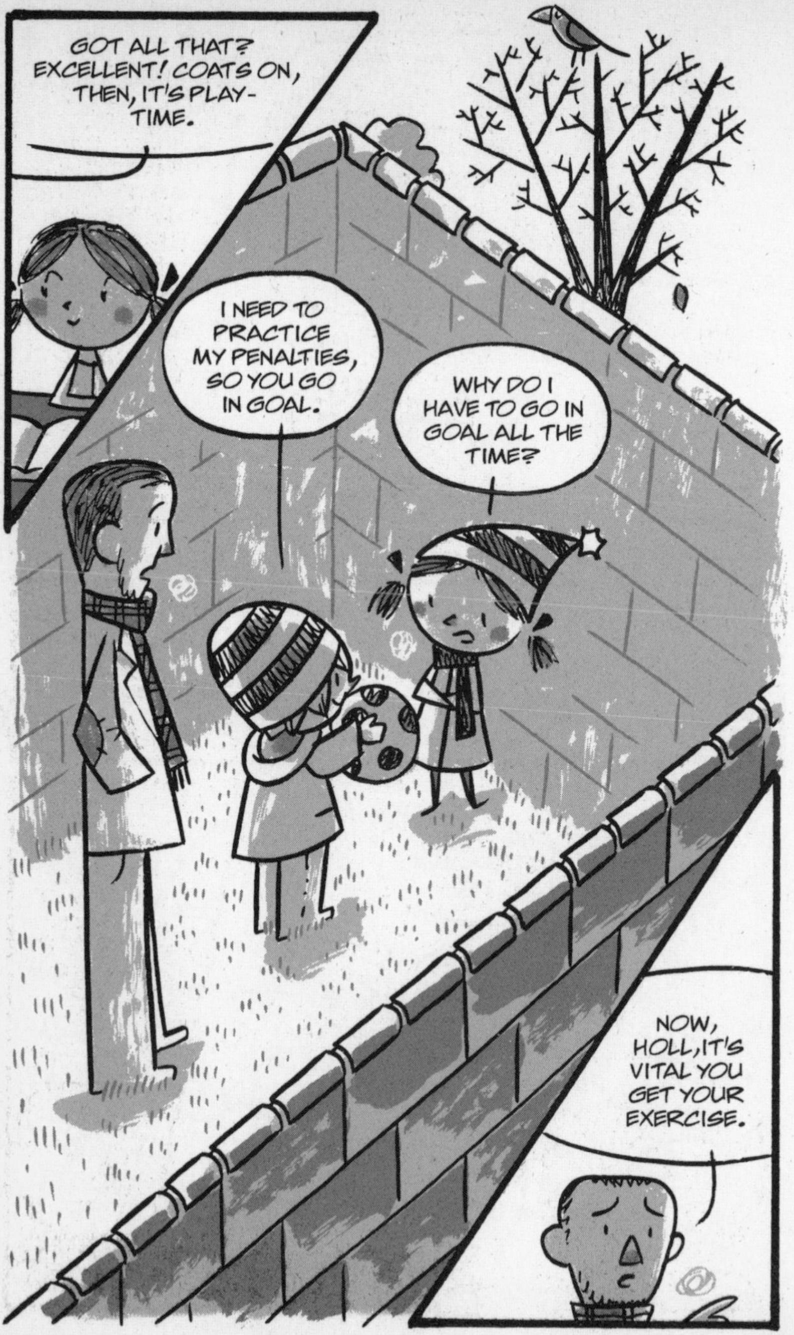
GOT ALL THAT? EXCELLENT! COATS ON, THEN, IT'S PLAY-TIME.
I NEED TO PRACTICE MY PENALTIES, SO YOU GO IN GOAL.
WHY DO I HAVE TO GO IN GOAL ALL THE TIME?
NOW, HOLL, IT'S VITAL YOU GET YOUR EXERCISE.

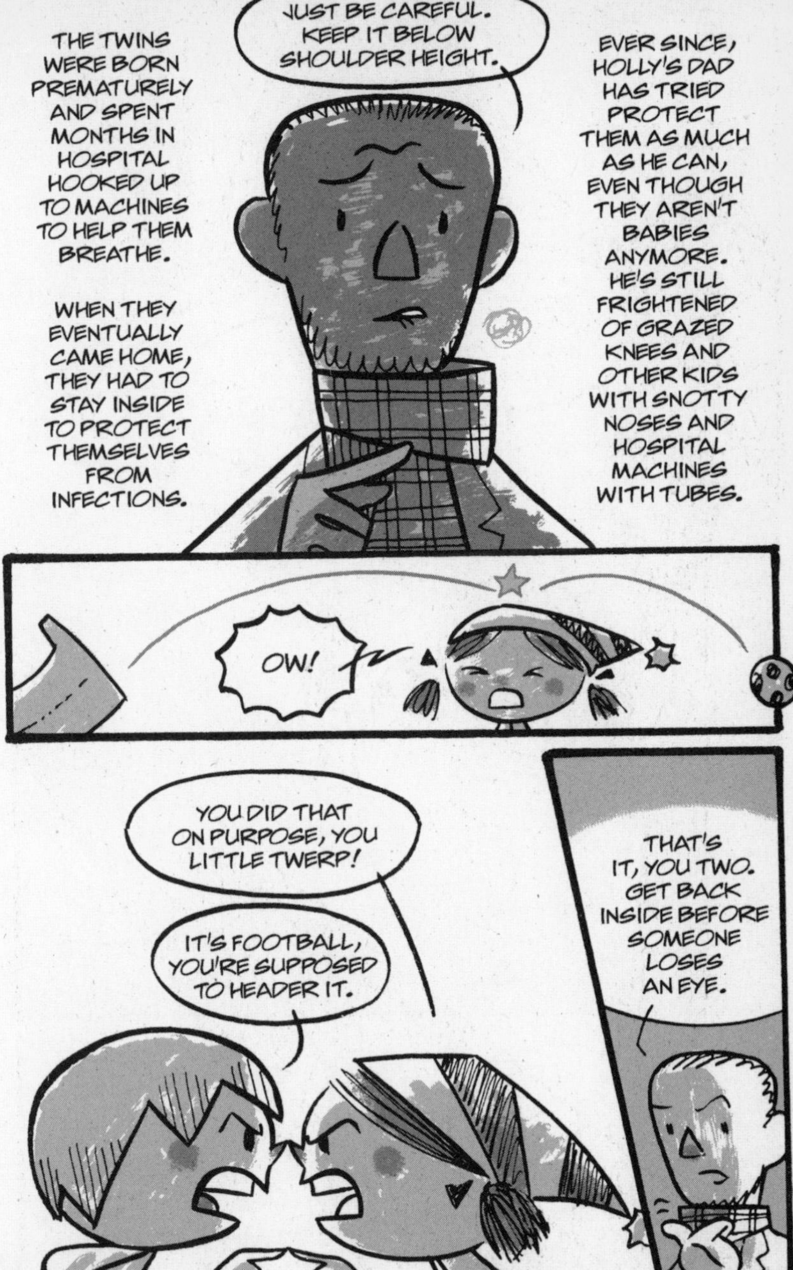
THE TWINS WERE BORN PREMATURELY AND SPENT MONTHS IN HOSPITAL HOOKED UP TO MACHINES TO HELP THEM BREATHE.
WHEN THEY EVENTUALLY CAME HOME, THEY HAD TO STAY INSIDE TO PROTECT THEMSELVES FROM INFECTIONS.
JUST BE CAREFUL. KEEP IT BELOW SHOULDER HEIGHT.
EVER SINCE, HOLLY'S DAD HAS TRIED PROTECT THEM AS MUCH AS HE CAN, EVEN THOUGH THEY AREN'T BABIES ANYMORE. HE'S STILL FRIGHTENED OF GRAZED KNEES AND OTHER KIDS WITH SNOTTY NOSES AND HOSPITAL MACHINES WITH TUBES.
OW!
YOU DID THAT ON PURPOSE, YOU LITTLE TWERP!
IT'S FOOTBALL, YOU'RE SUPPOSED TO HEADER IT.
THAT'S IT, YOU TWO. GET BACK INSIDE BEFORE SOMEONE LOSES AN EYE.

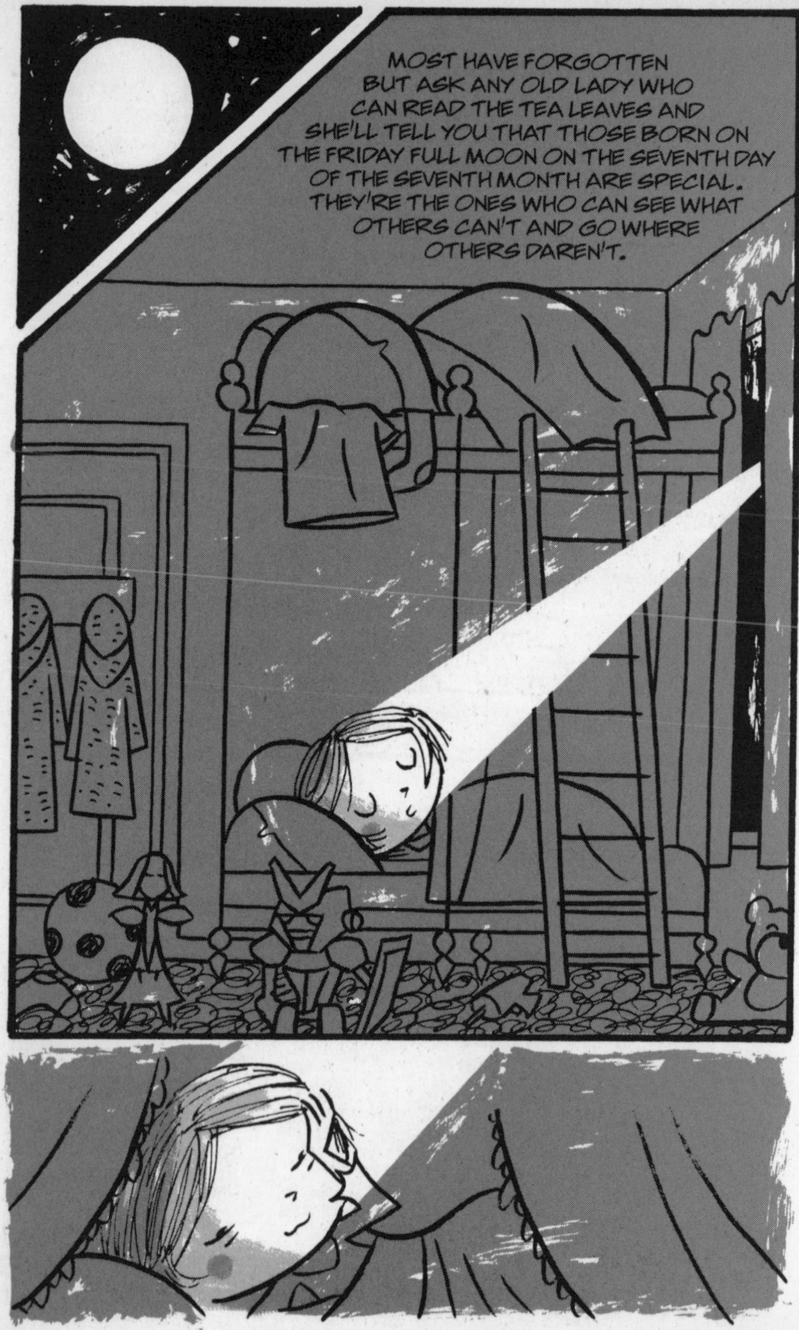
MOST HAVE FORGOTTEN BUT ASK ANY OLD LADY WHO CAN READ THE TEA LEAVES AND SHE'LL TELL YOU THAT THOSE BORN ON THE FRIDAY FULL MOON ON THE SEVENTH DAY OF THE SEVENTH MONTH ARE SPECIAL. THEY'RE THE ONES WHO CAN SEE WHAT OTHERS CAN'T AND GO WHERE OTHERS DAREN'T.

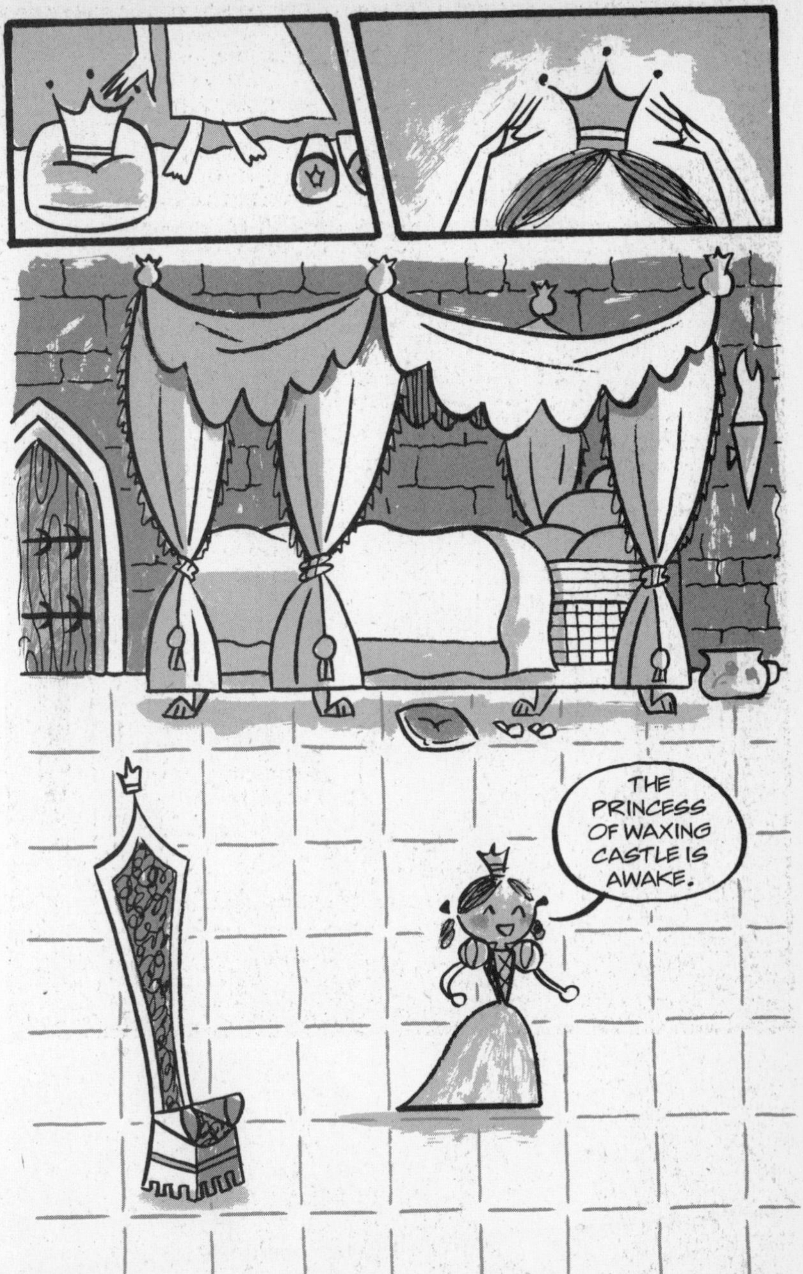
THE PRINCESS OF WAXING CASTLE IS AWAKE.

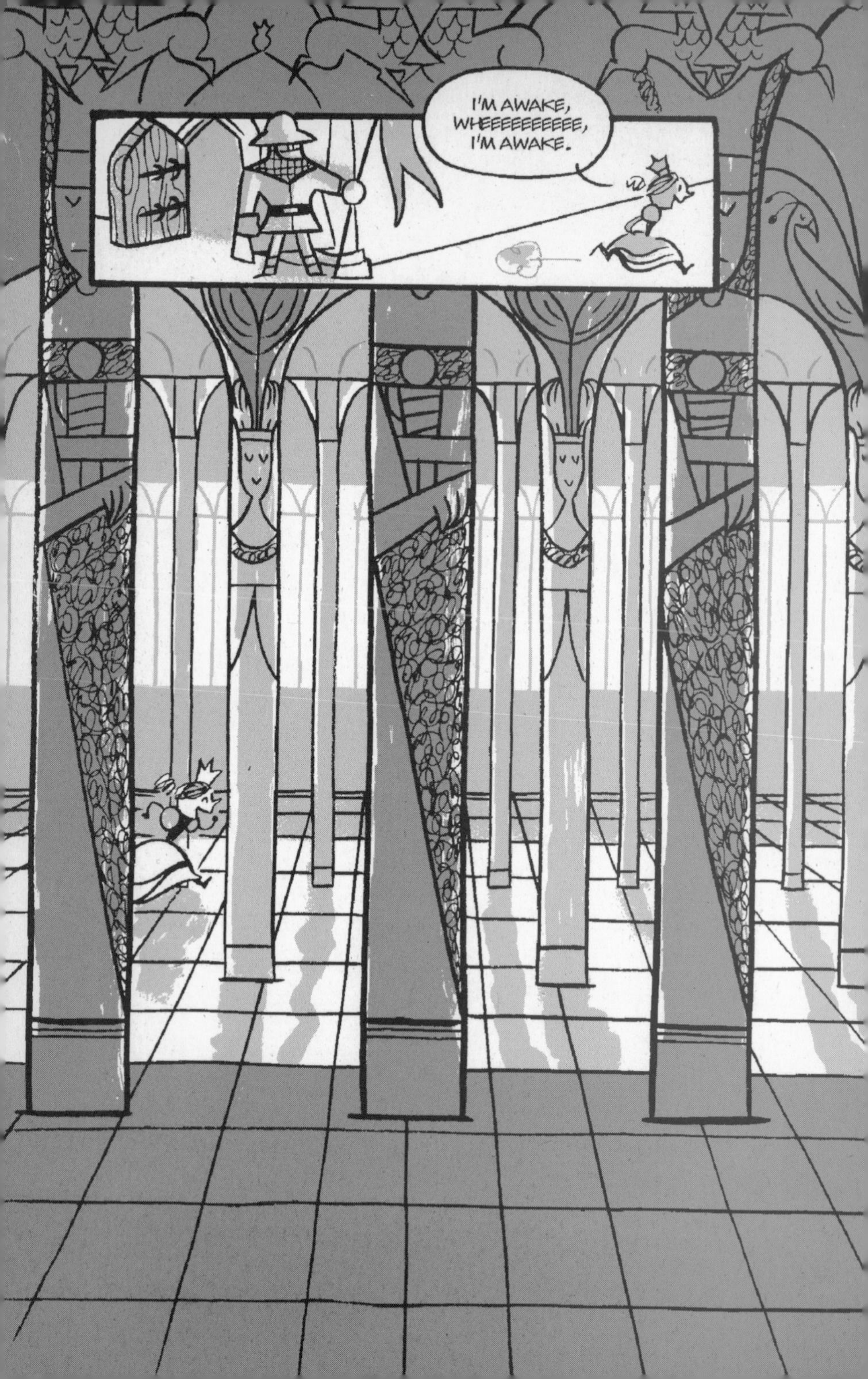
I'M AWAKE, WHEEEEEEEEEE, I'M AWAKE.

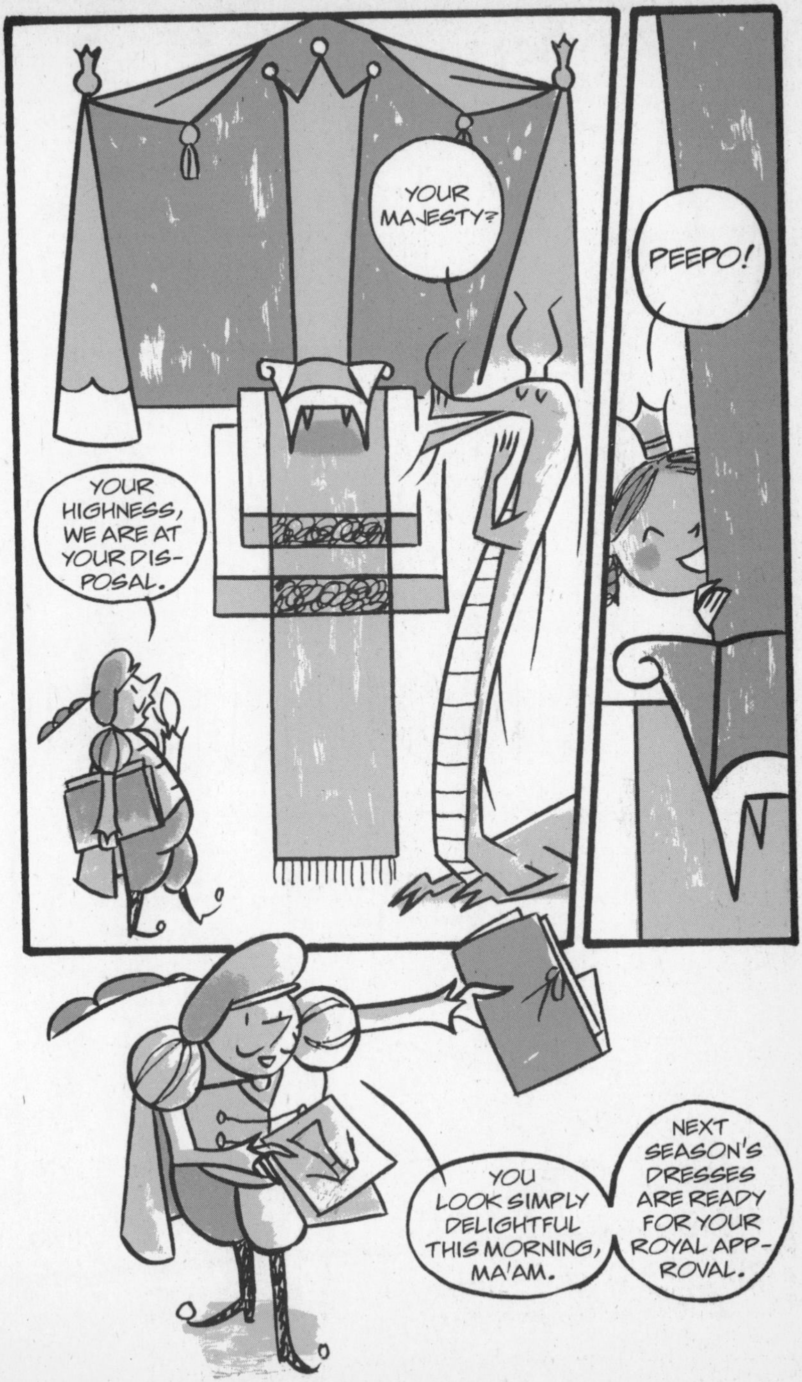
YOUR MAJESTY?
YOUR HIGHNESS, WE ARE AT YOUR DIS-POSAL.
PEEPO!
YOU LOOK SIMPLY DELIGHTFUL THIS MORNING, MA'AM.
NEXT SEASON'S DRESSES ARE READY FOR YOUR ROYAL APP-ROVAL.

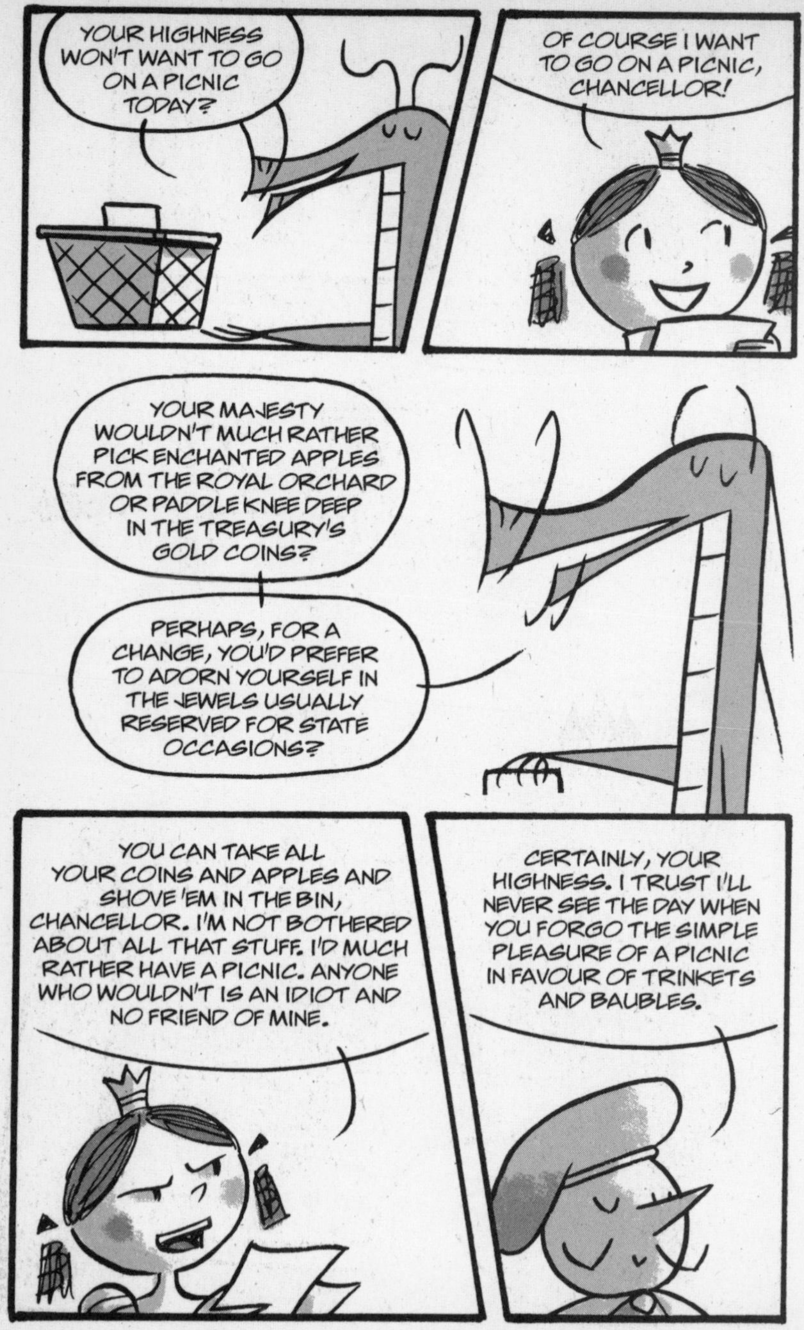
YOUR HIGHNESS WON'T WANT TO GO ON A PICNIC TODAY?
OF COURSE I WANT TO GO ON A PICNIC, CHANCELLOR!
YOUR MAJESTY WOULDN'T MUCH RATHER PICK ENCHANTED APPLES FROM THE ROYAL ORCHARD OR PADDLE KNEE DEEP IN THE TREASURY'S GOLD COINS?
PERHAPS, FOR A CHANGE, YOU'D PREFER TO ADORN YOURSELF IN THE JEWELS USUALLY RESERVED FOR STATE OCCASIONS?
YOU CAN TAKE ALL YOUR COINS AND APPLES AND SHOVE 'EM IN THE BIN, CHANCELLOR. I'M NOT BOTHERED ABOUT ALL THAT STUFF. I'D MUCH RATHER HAVE A PICNIC. ANYONE WHO WOULDN'T IS AN IDIOT AND NO FRIEND OF MINE.
CERTAINLY, YOUR HIGHNESS. I TRUST I'LL NEVER SEE THE DAY WHEN YOU FORGO THE SIMPLE PLEASURE OF A PICNIC IN FAVOUR OF TRINKETS AND BAUBLES.

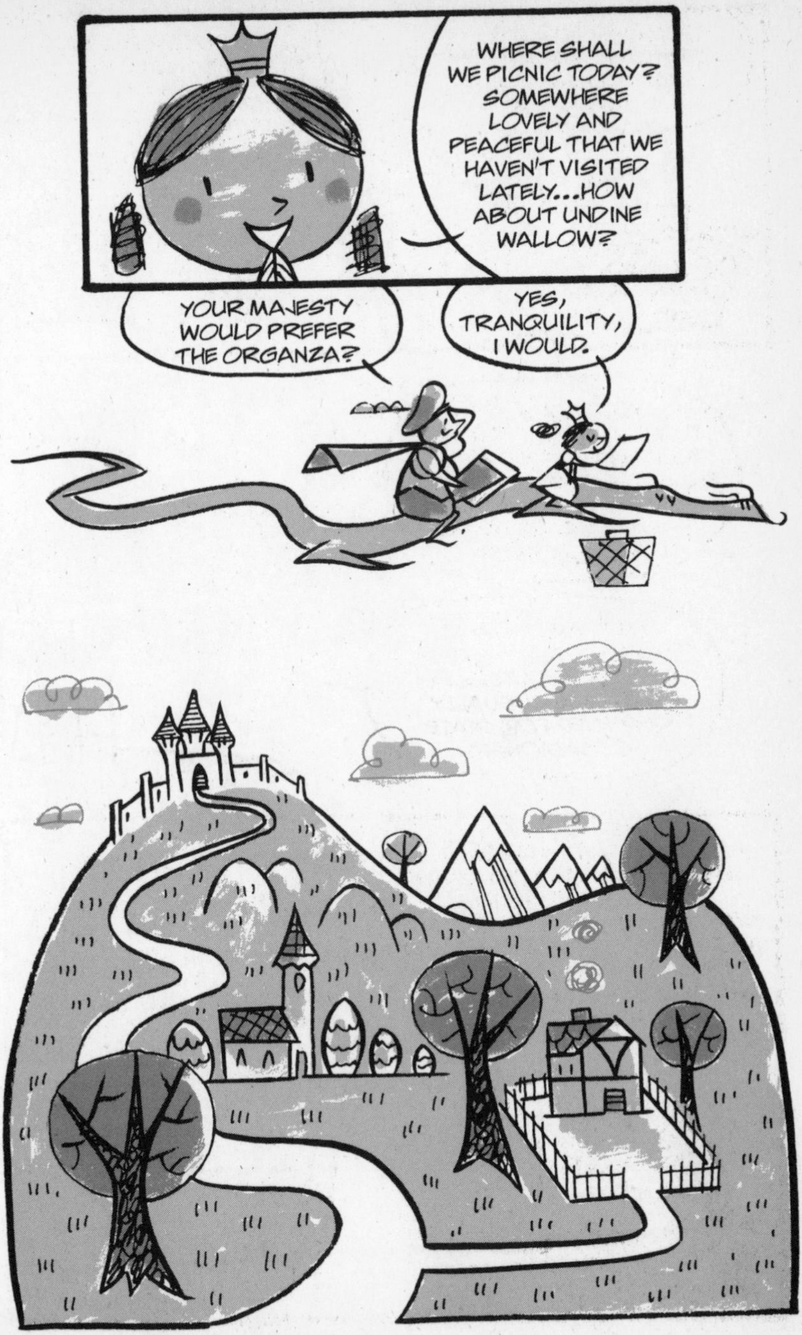
WHERE SHALL WE PICNIC TODAY? SOMEWHERE LOVELY AND PEACEFUL THAT WE HAVEN'T VISITED LATELY...HOW ABOUT UNDINE WALLOW?
YOUR MAJESTY WOULD PREFER THE ORGANZA?
YES, TRANQUILITY, I WOULD.

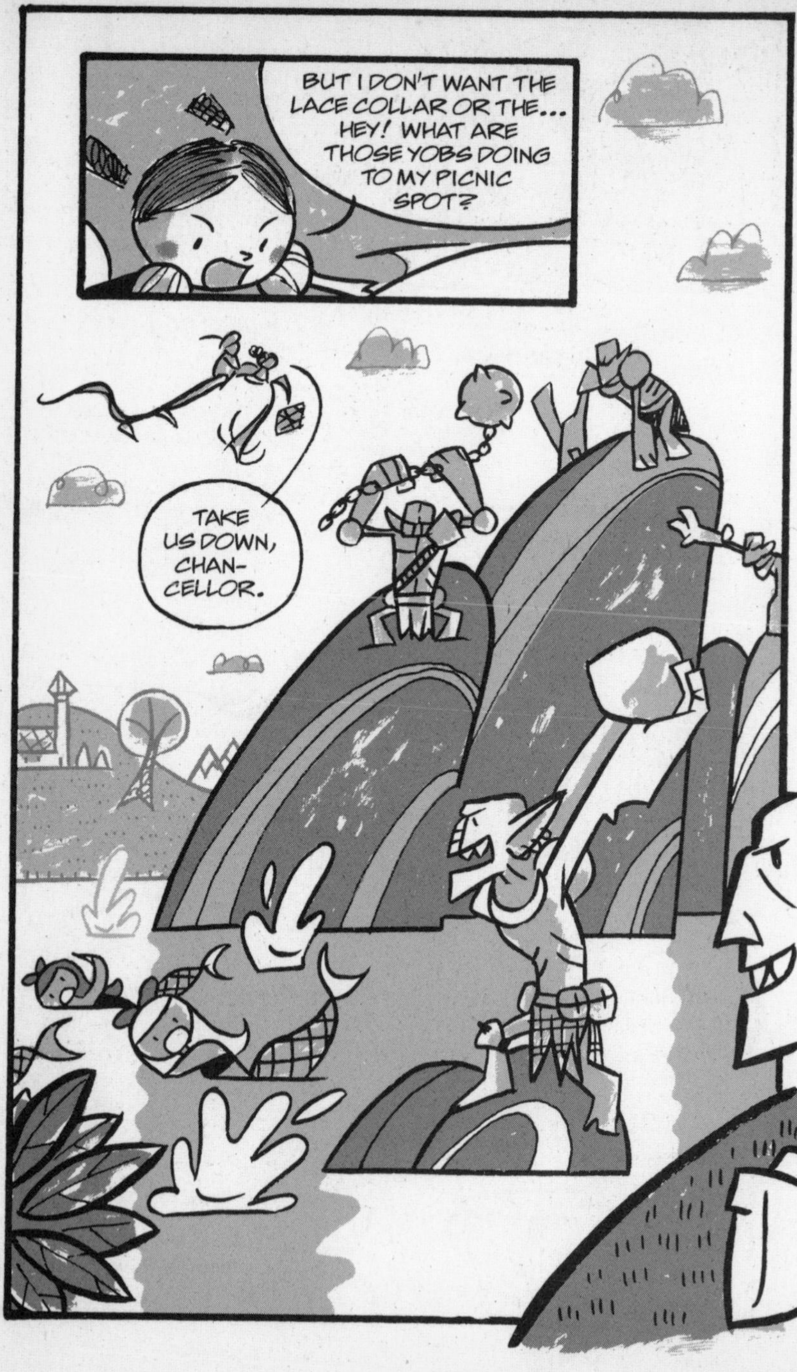

BUT I DON'T WANT THE LACE COLLAR OR THE... HEY! WHAT ARE THOSE YOBS DOING TO MY PICNIC SPOT?
TAKE US DOWN, CHAN-CELLOR.

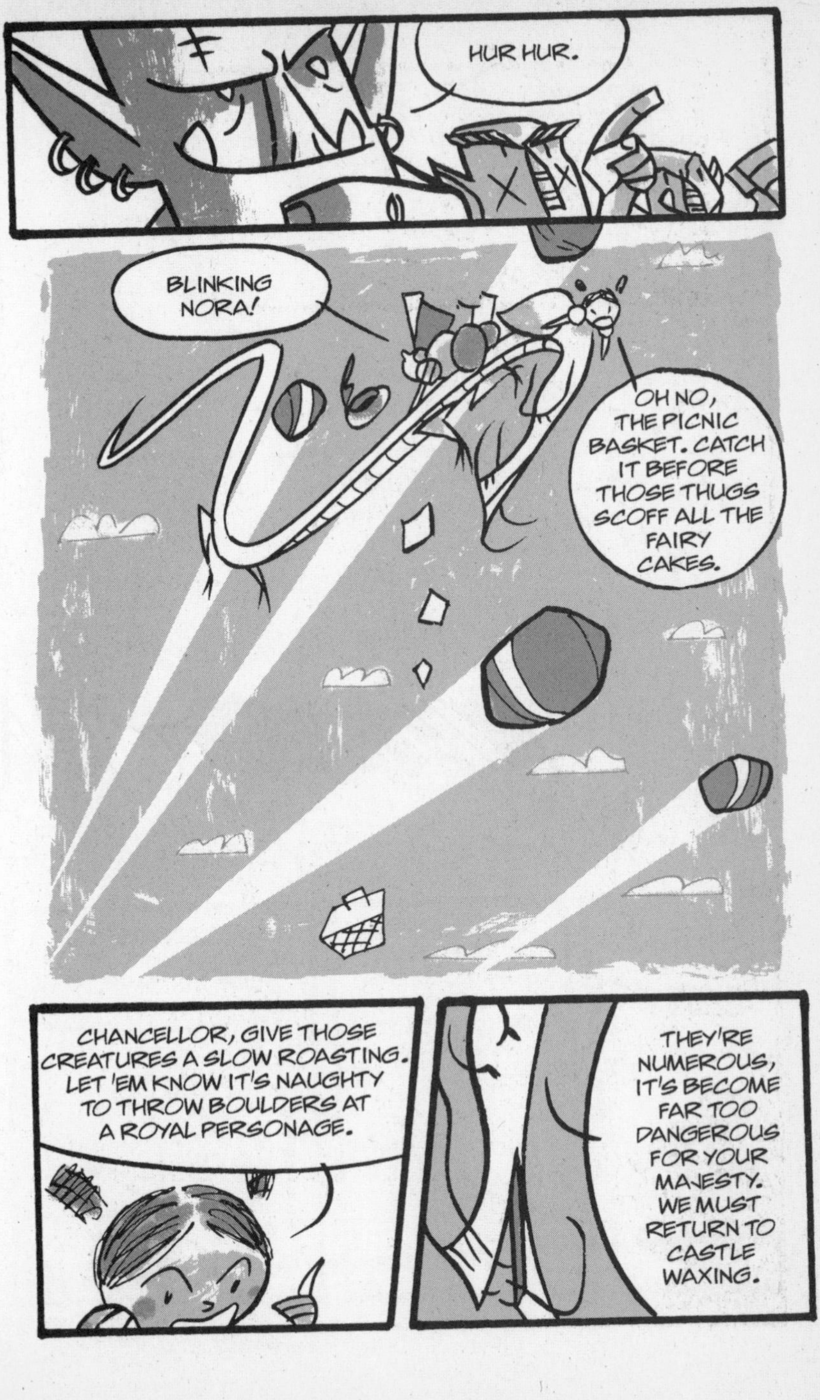
HUR HUR.
BLINKING NORA!
OH NO, THE PICNIC BASKET. CATCH IT BEFORE THOSE THUGS SCOFF ALL THE FAIRY CAKES.
CHANCELLOR, GIVE THOSE CREATURES A SLOW ROASTING. LET 'EM KNOW IT'S NAUGHTY TO THROW BOULDERS AT A ROYAL PERSONAGE.
THEY'RE NUMEROUS, IT'S BECOME FAR TOO DANGEROUS FOR YOUR MAJESTY. WE MUST RETURN TO CASTLE WAXING.

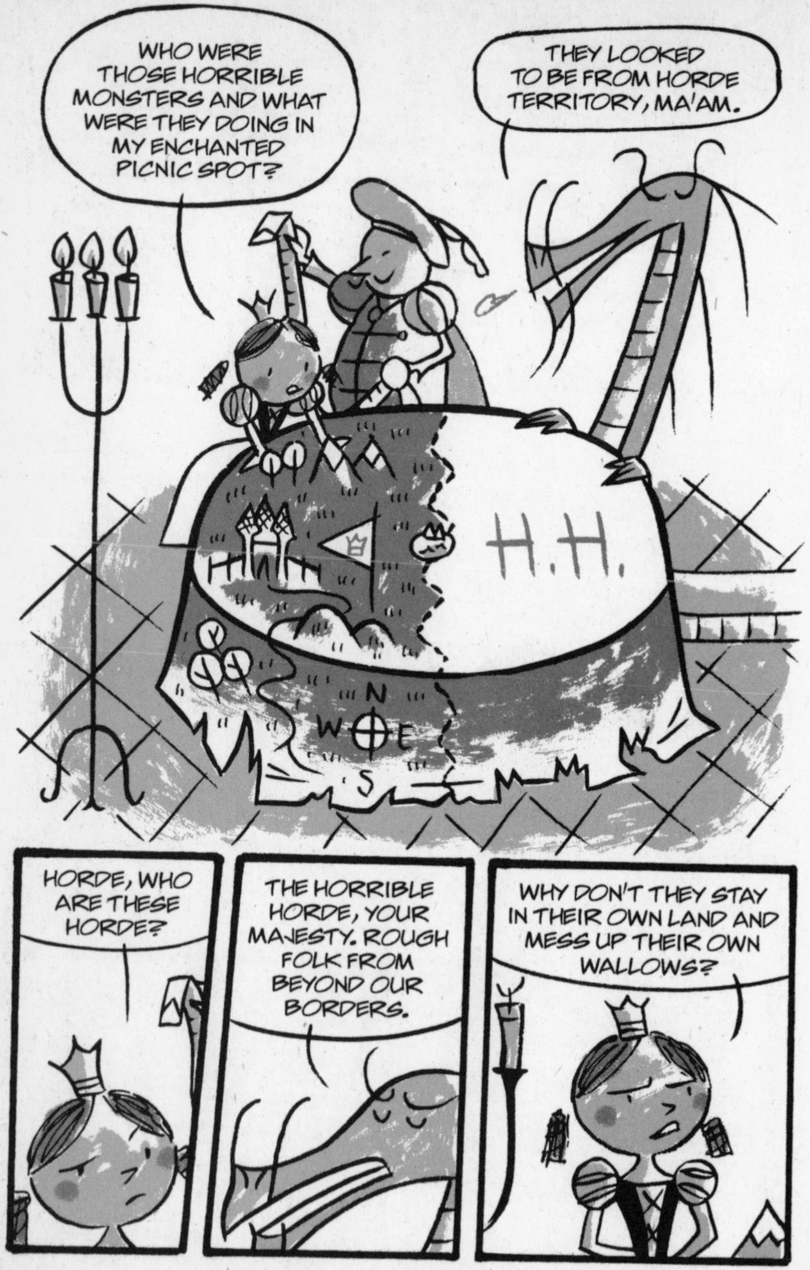
WHO WERE THOSE HORRIBLE MONSTERS AND WHAT WERE THEY DOING IN MY ENCHANTED PICNIC SPOT?
THEY LOOKED TO BE FROM HORDE TERRITORY, MA'AM.
H.H.
N
W
E
S
HORDE, WHO ARE THESE HORDE?
THE HORRIBLE HORDE, YOUR MAJESTY. ROUGH FOLK FROM BEYOND OUR BORDERS.
WHY DON'T THEY STAY IN THEIR OWN LAND AND MESS UP THEIR OWN WALLOWS?

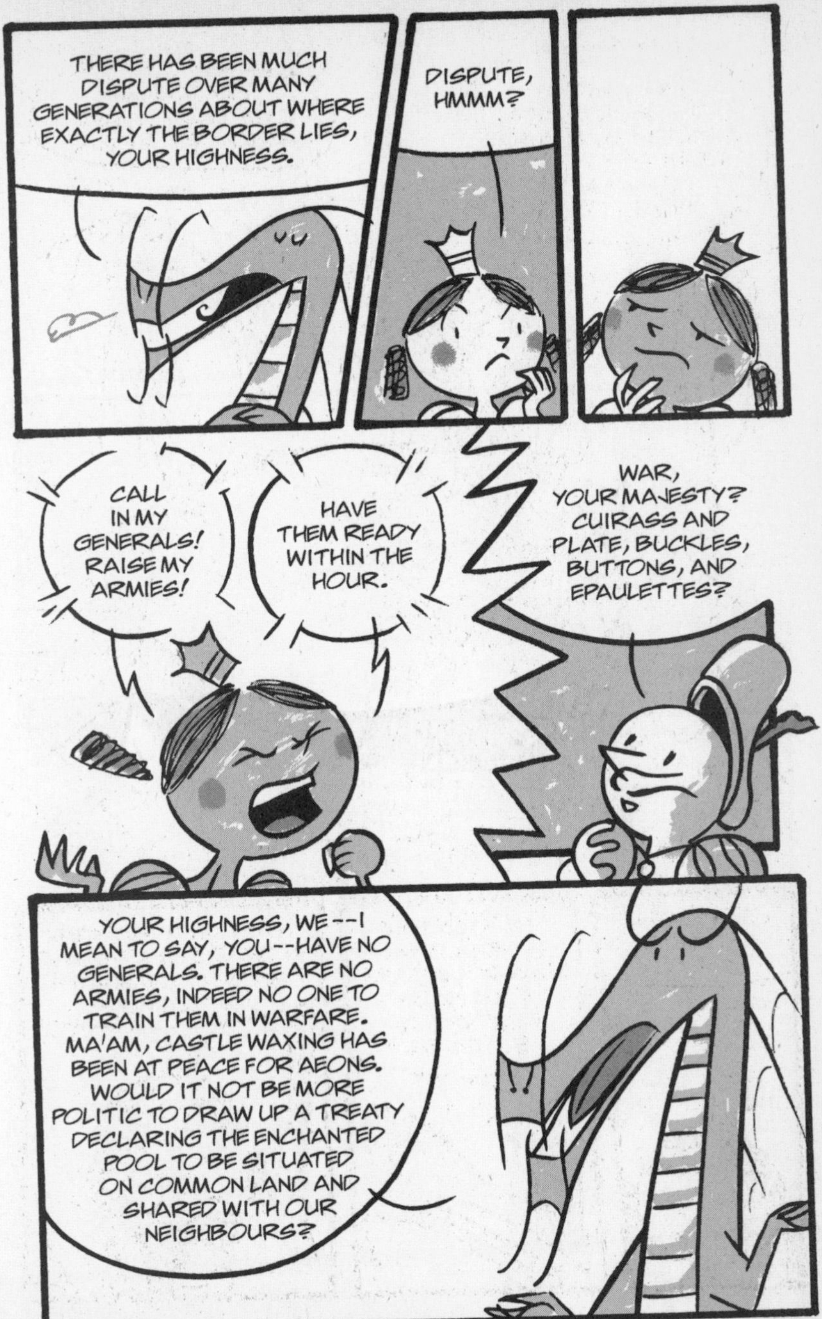
THERE HAS BEEN MUCH DISPUTE OVER MANY GENERATIONS ABOUT WHERE EXACTLY THE BORDER LIES, YOUR HIGHNESS.
DISPUTE, HMMM?
CALL IN MY GENERALS! RAISE MY ARMIES!
HAVE THEM READY WITHIN THE HOUR.
WAR, YOUR MAJESTY? CUIRASS AND PLATE, BUCKLES, BUTTONS, AND EPAULETTES?
YOUR HIGHNESS, WE--I MEAN TO SAY, YOU--HAVE NO GENERALS. THERE ARE NO ARMIES, INDEED NO ONE TO TRAIN THEM IN WARFARE. MA'AM, CASTLE WAXING HAS BEEN AT PEACE FOR AEONS. WOULD IT NOT BE MORE POLITIC TO DRAW UP A TREATY DECLARING THE ENCHANTED POOL TO BE SITUATED ON COMMON LAND AND SHARED WITH OUR NEIGHBOURS?

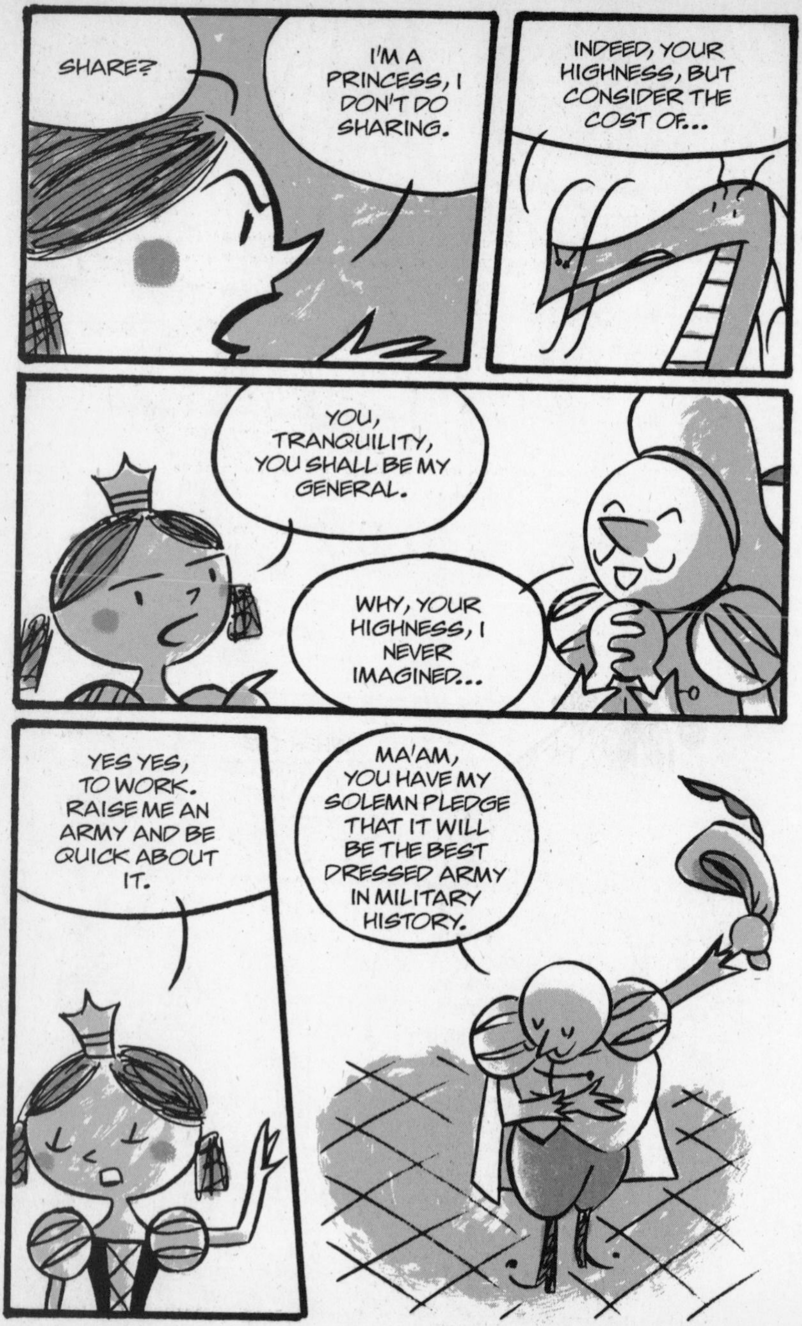
SHARE?
I'M A PRINCESS, I DON'T DO SHARING.
INDEED, YOUR HIGHNESS, BUT CONSIDER THE COST OF...
YOU, TRANQUILITY, YOU SHALL BE MY GENERAL.
WHY, YOUR HIGHNESS, I NEVER IMAGINED...
YES YES, TO WORK. RAISE ME AN ARMY AND BE QUICK ABOUT IT.
MA'AM, YOU HAVE MY SOLEMN PLEDGE THAT IT WILL BE THE BEST DRESSED ARMY IN MILITARY HISTORY.

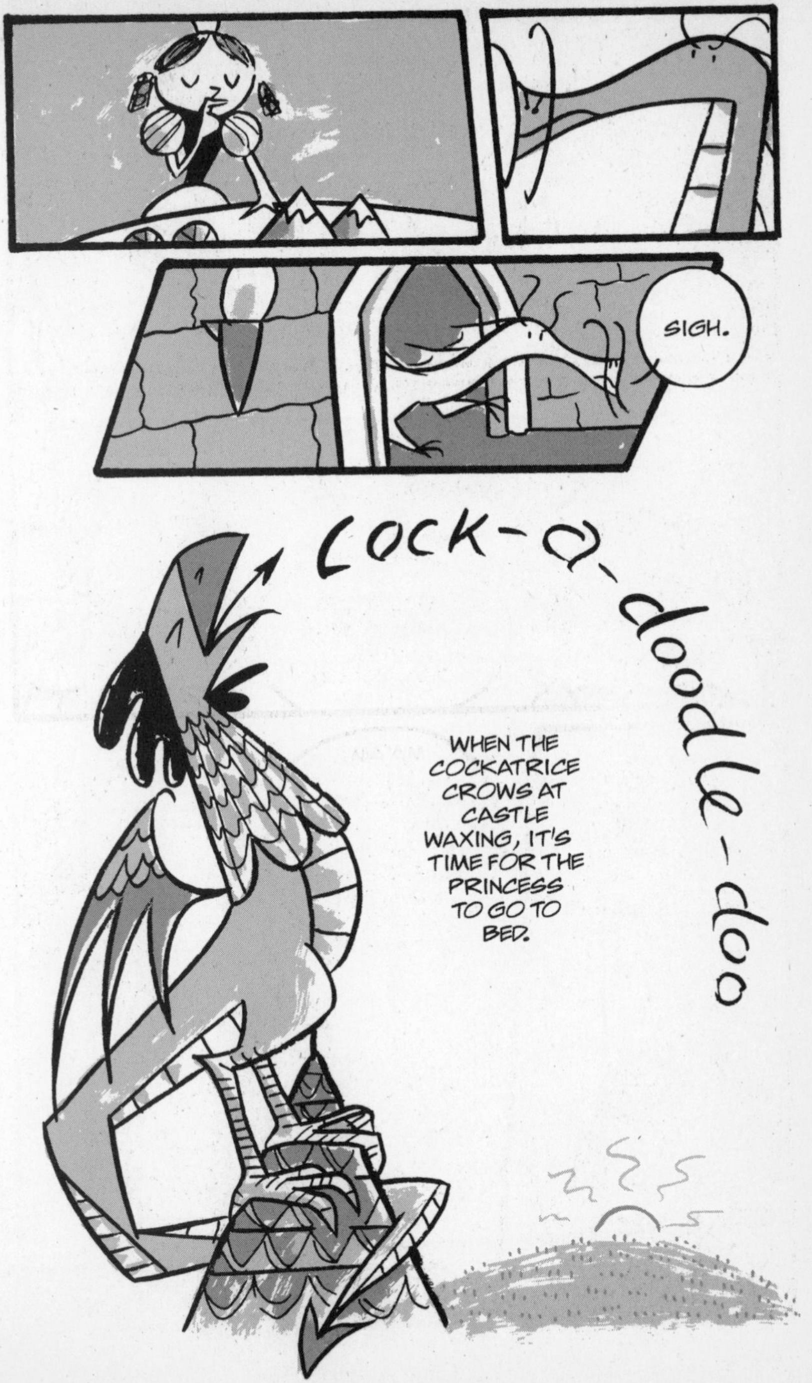
SIGH.
COCK-A-DOODLE-DOO
WHEN THE COCKATRICE CROWS AT CASTLE WAXING, IT'S TIME FOR THE PRINCESS TO GO TO BED.

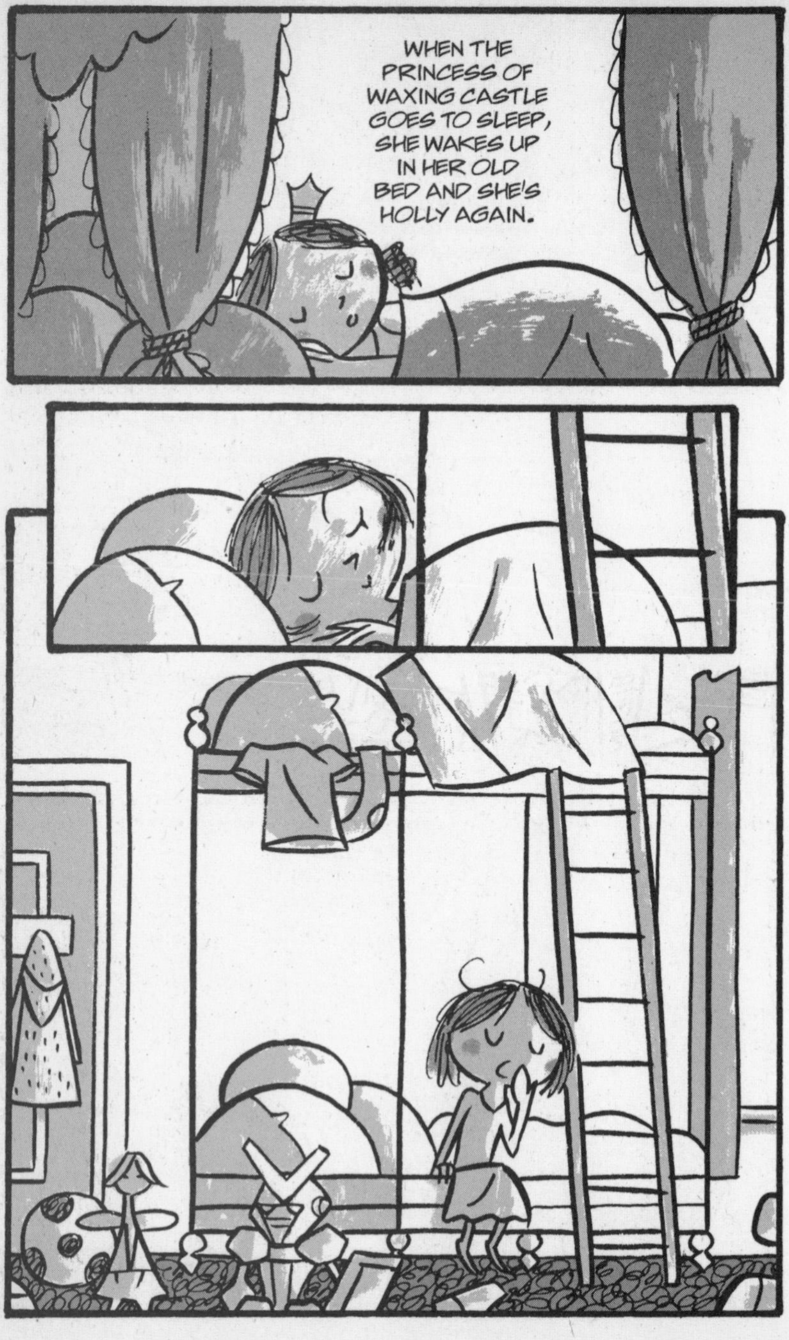
WHEN THE PRINCESS OF WAXING CASTLE GOES TO SLEEP, SHE WAKES UP IN HER OLD BED AND SHE'S HOLLY AGAIN.

HOLLY'S MIND ISN'T REALLY ON SCHOOL-WORK, SHE'S ALREADY THINKING AND PLANNING AHEAD FOR THE NIGHT.

THAT'S RIGHT, HOLL. YOU GO IN GOAL.

QUALITY SAVE, SIS.

"HE W... FEARS B... CONQUERED... OF DEFEA..."

THAT'S IT, YOU TWO. INSIDE.

"TAKE TIME TO DELIBERATE, BUT WHEN THE TIME FOR ACTION HAS ARRIVED, STOP THINKING AND GO IN."

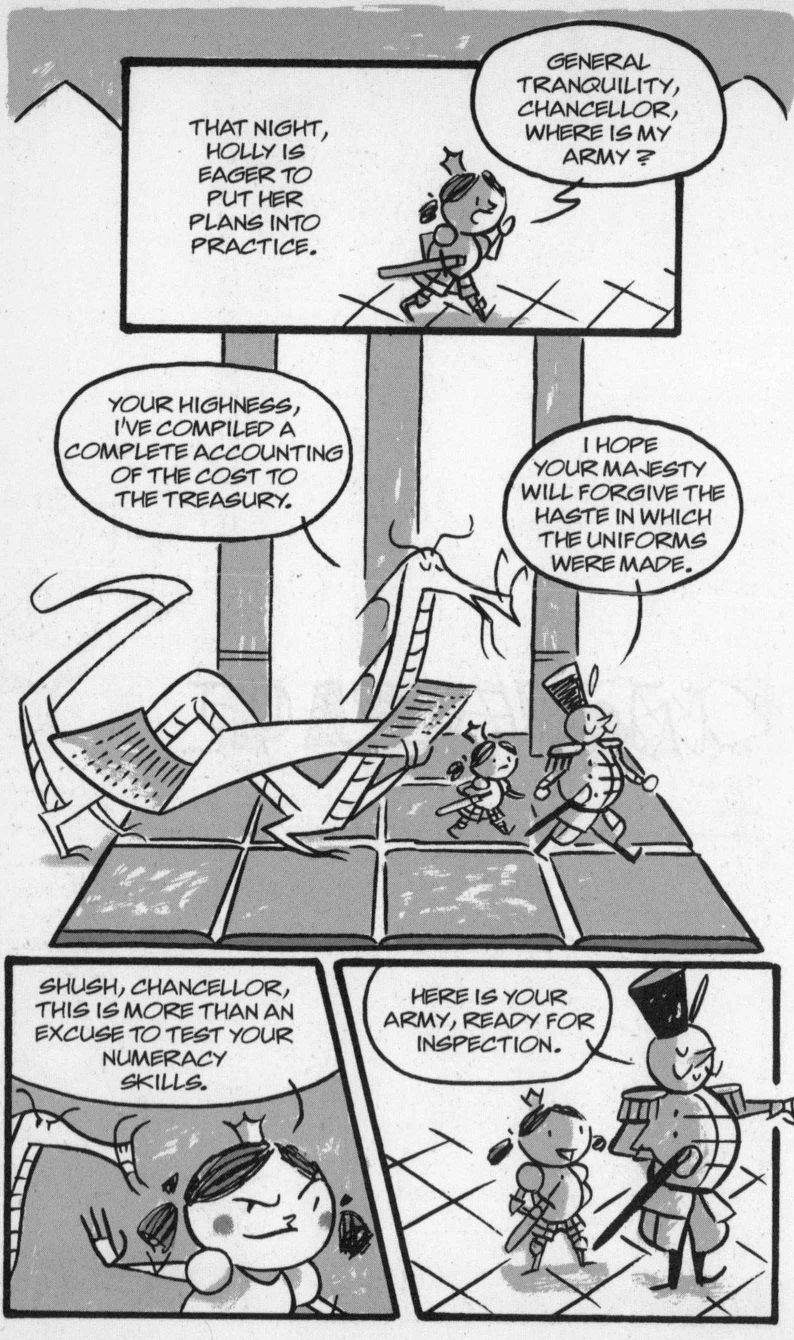
THAT NIGHT, HOLLY IS EAGER TO PUT HER PLANS INTO PRACTICE.
GENERAL TRANQUILITY, CHANCELLOR, WHERE IS MY ARMY ?
YOUR HIGHNESS, I'VE COMPILED A COMPLETE ACCOUNTING OF THE COST TO THE TREASURY.
I HOPE YOUR MAJESTY WILL FORGIVE THE HASTE IN WHICH THE UNIFORMS WERE MADE.
SHUSH, CHANCELLOR, THIS IS MORE THAN AN EXCUSE TO TEST YOUR NUMERACY SKILLS.
HERE IS YOUR ARMY, READY FOR INSPECTION.

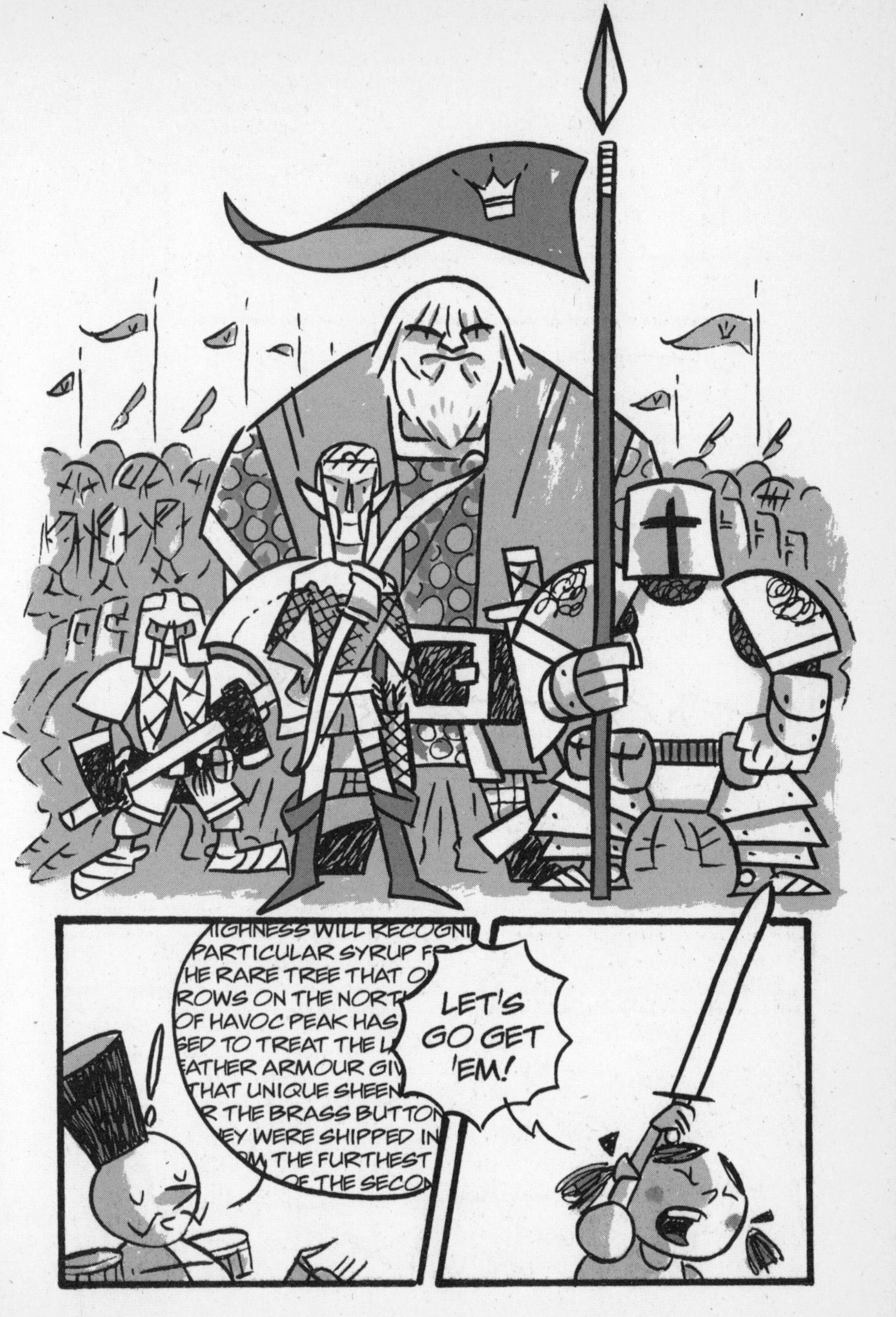
IGHNESS WILL RECOGNI PARTICULAR SYRUP FR HE RARE TREE THAT O ROWS ON THE NORT OF HAVOC PEAK HAS SED TO TREAT THE L EATHER ARMOUR GIV THAT UNIQUE SHEEN R THE BRASS BUTTON EY WERE SHIPPED IN OM THE FURTHEST OF THE SECO
LET'S GO GET 'EM!

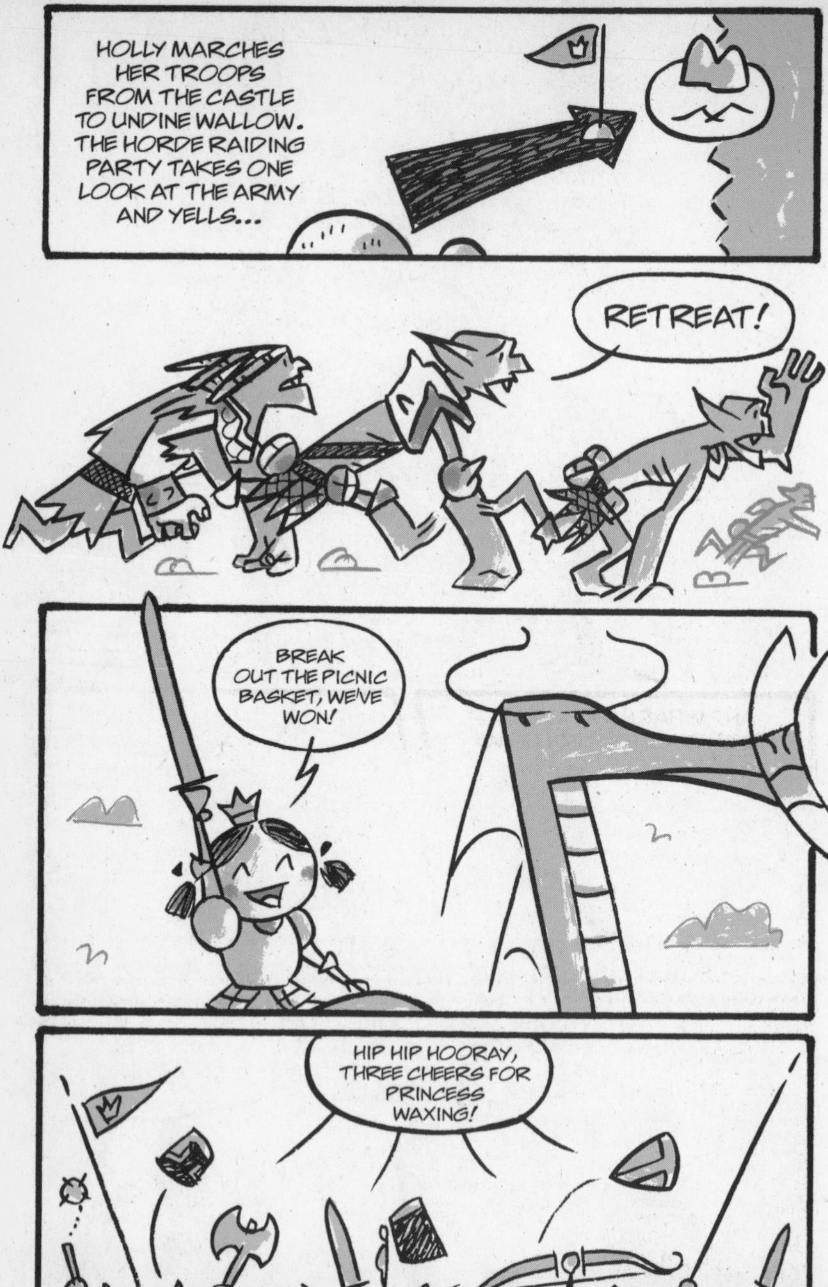
HOLLY MARCHES HER TROOPS FROM THE CASTLE TO UNDINE WALLOW. THE HORDE RAIDING PARTY TAKES ONE LOOK AT THE ARMY AND YELLS...
RETREAT!
BREAK OUT THE PICNIC BASKET, WE'VE WON!
HIP HIP HOORAY, THREE CHEERS FOR PRINCESS WAXING!

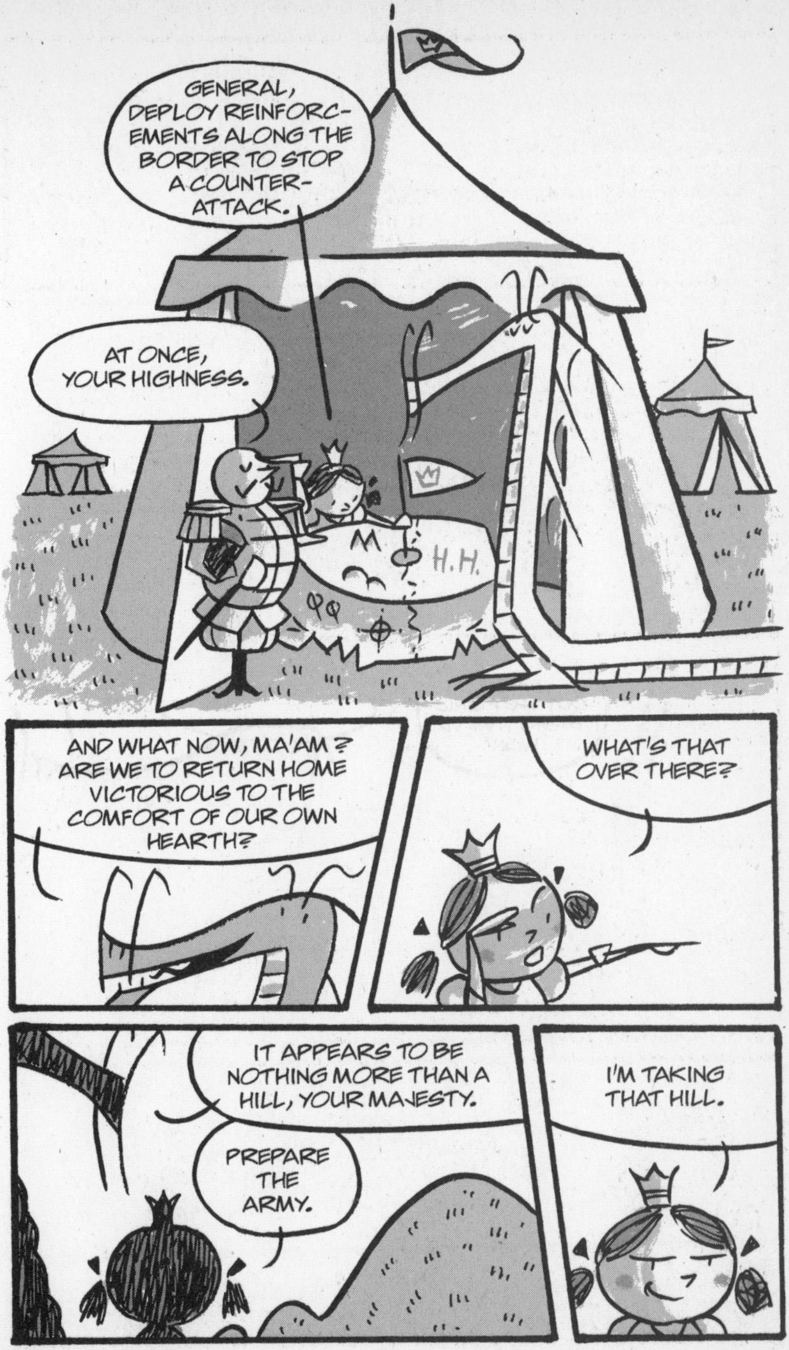
GENERAL, DEPLOY REINFORCEMENTS ALONG THE BORDER TO STOP A COUNTER-ATTACK.
AT ONCE, YOUR HIGHNESS.
AND WHAT NOW, MA'AM? ARE WE TO RETURN HOME VICTORIOUS TO THE COMFORT OF OUR OWN HEARTH?
WHAT'S THAT OVER THERE?
IT APPEARS TO BE NOTHING MORE THAN A HILL, YOUR MAJESTY.
PREPARE THE ARMY.
I'M TAKING THAT HILL.
M
H.H.

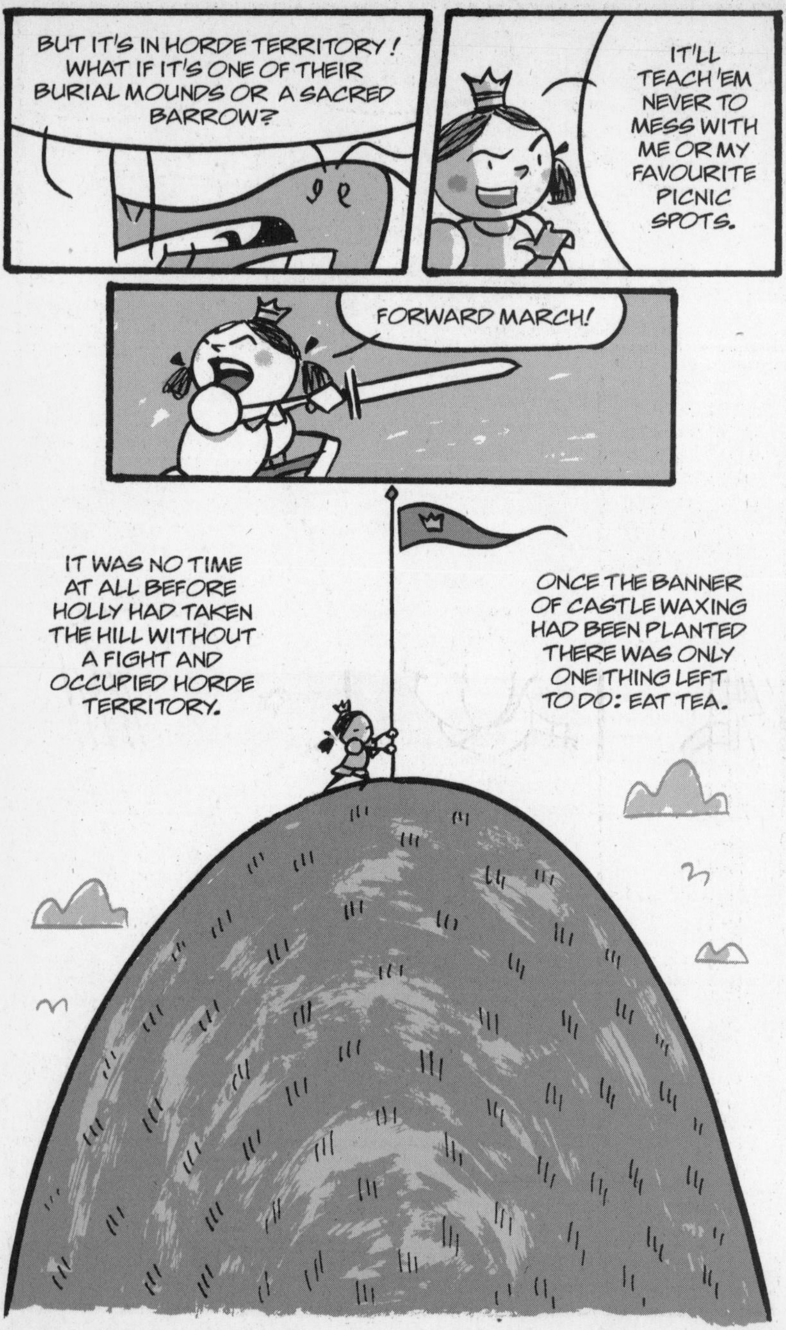

BUT IT'S IN HORDE TERRITORY! WHAT IF IT'S ONE OF THEIR BURIAL MOUNDS OR A SACRED BARROW?
IT'LL TEACH 'EM NEVER TO MESS WITH ME OR MY FAVOURITE PICNIC SPOTS.
FORWARD MARCH!
IT WAS NO TIME AT ALL BEFORE HOLLY HAD TAKEN THE HILL WITHOUT A FIGHT AND OCCUPIED HORDE TERRITORY.
ONCE THE BANNER OF CASTLE WAXING HAD BEEN PLANTED THERE WAS ONLY ONE THING LEFT TO DO: EAT TEA.

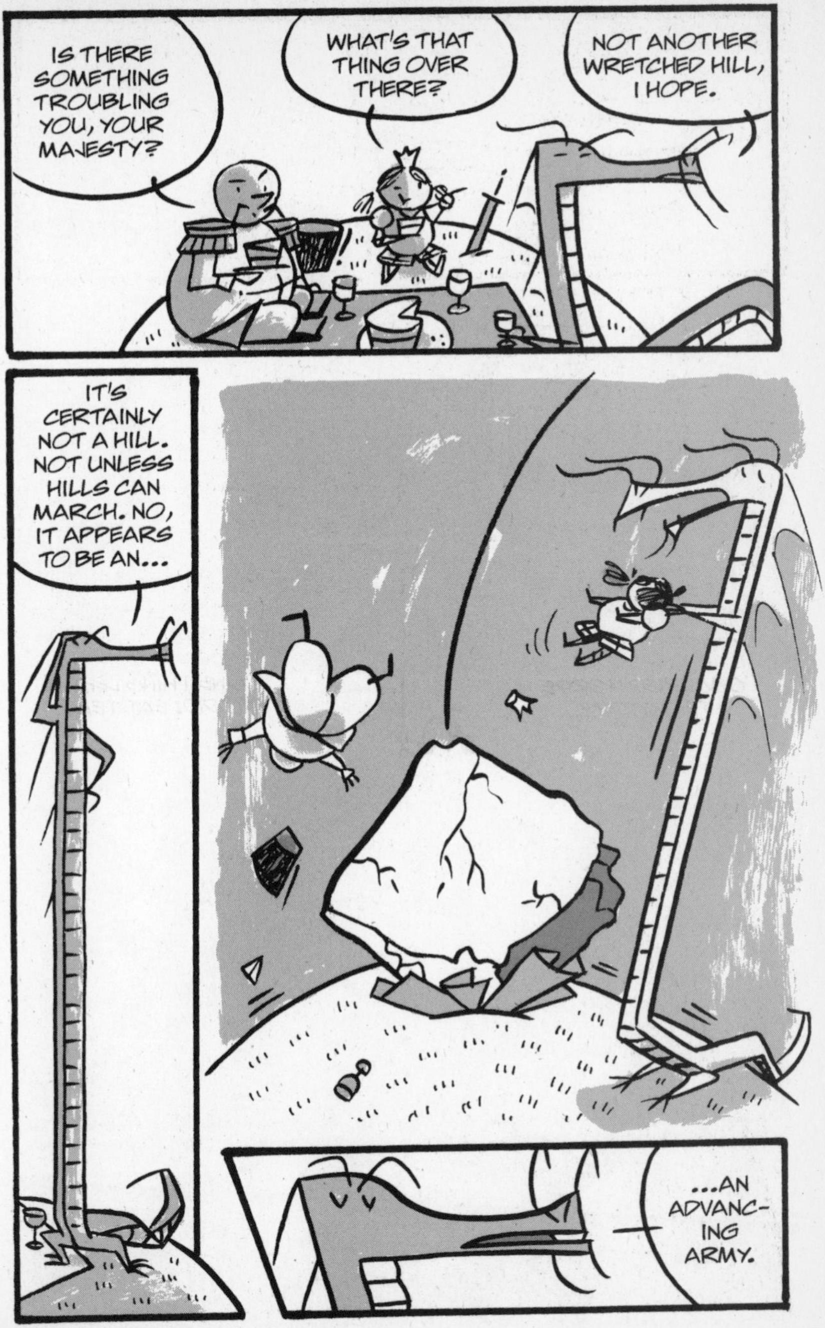
IS THERE SOMETHING TROUBLING YOU, YOUR MAJESTY?
WHAT'S THAT THING OVER THERE?
NOT ANOTHER WRETCHED HILL, I HOPE.
IT'S CERTAINLY NOT A HILL. NOT UNLESS HILLS CAN MARCH. NO, IT APPEARS TO BE AN...
...AN ADVANC-ING ARMY.

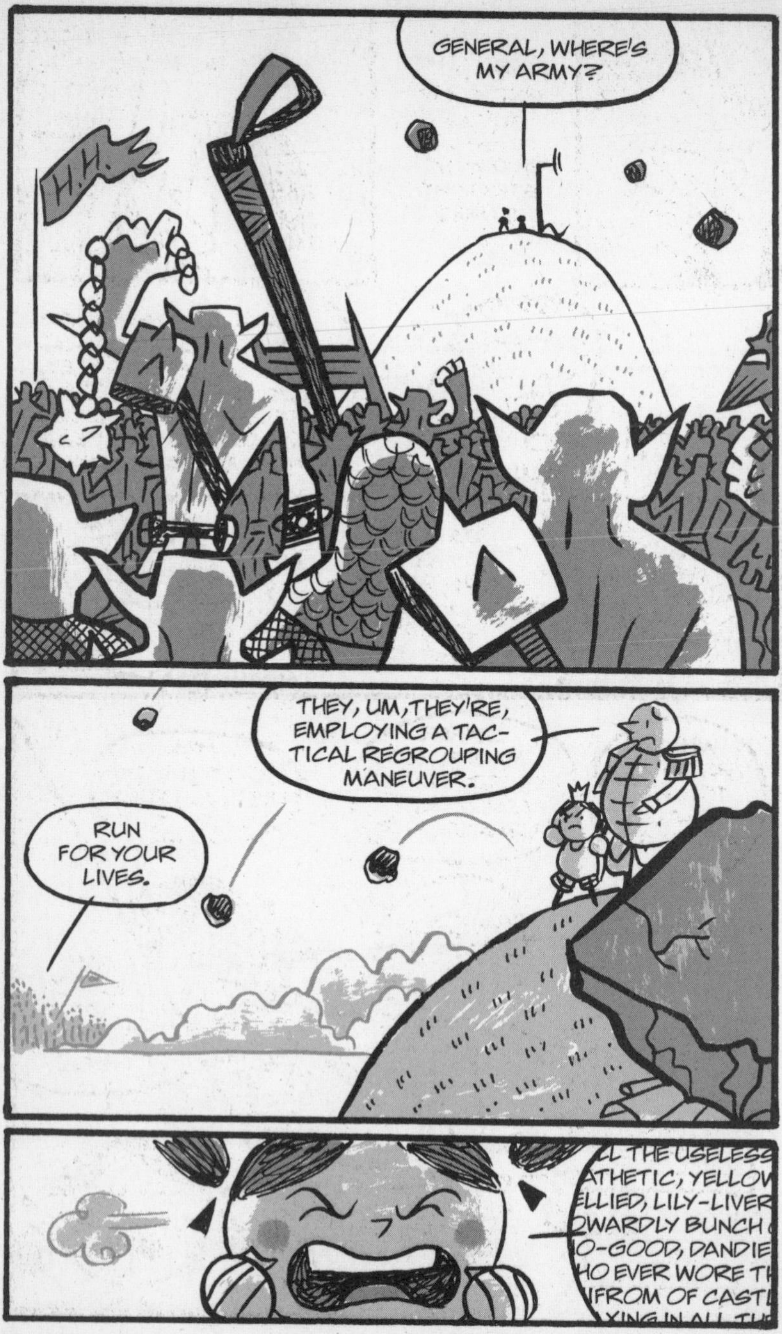
GENERAL, WHERE'S MY ARMY?
H.H.
THEY, UM, THEY'RE, EMPLOYING A TAC-TICAL REGROUPING MANEUVER.
RUN FOR YOUR LIVES.
LL THE USELESS
ATHETIC, YELLOW
ELLIED, LILY-LIVER
OWARDLY BUNCH
O-GOOD, DANDIE
HO EVER WORE TH

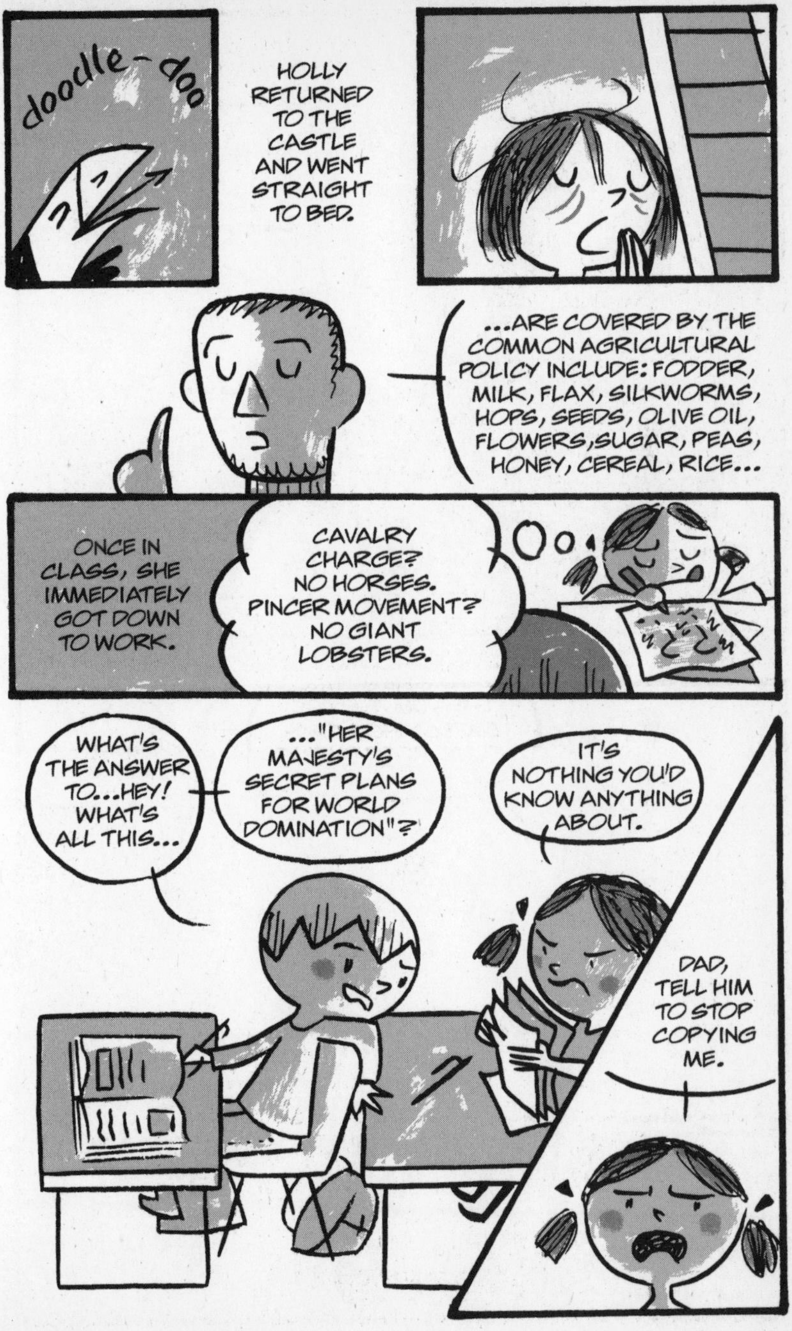
doodle-doo
HOLLY RETURNED TO THE CASTLE AND WENT STRAIGHT TO BED.
...ARE COVERED BY THE COMMON AGRICULTURAL POLICY INCLUDE: FODDER, MILK, FLAX, SILKWORMS, HOPS, SEEDS, OLIVE OIL, FLOWERS, SUGAR, PEAS, HONEY, CEREAL, RICE...
ONCE IN CLASS, SHE IMMEDIATELY GOT DOWN TO WORK.
CAVALRY CHARGE? NO HORSES. PINCER MOVEMENT? NO GIANT LOBSTERS.
WHAT'S THE ANSWER TO...HEY! WHAT'S ALL THIS...
..."HER MAJESTY'S SECRET PLANS FOR WORLD DOMINATION"?
IT'S NOTHING YOU'D KNOW ANYTHING ABOUT.
DAD, TELL HIM TO STOP COPYING ME.

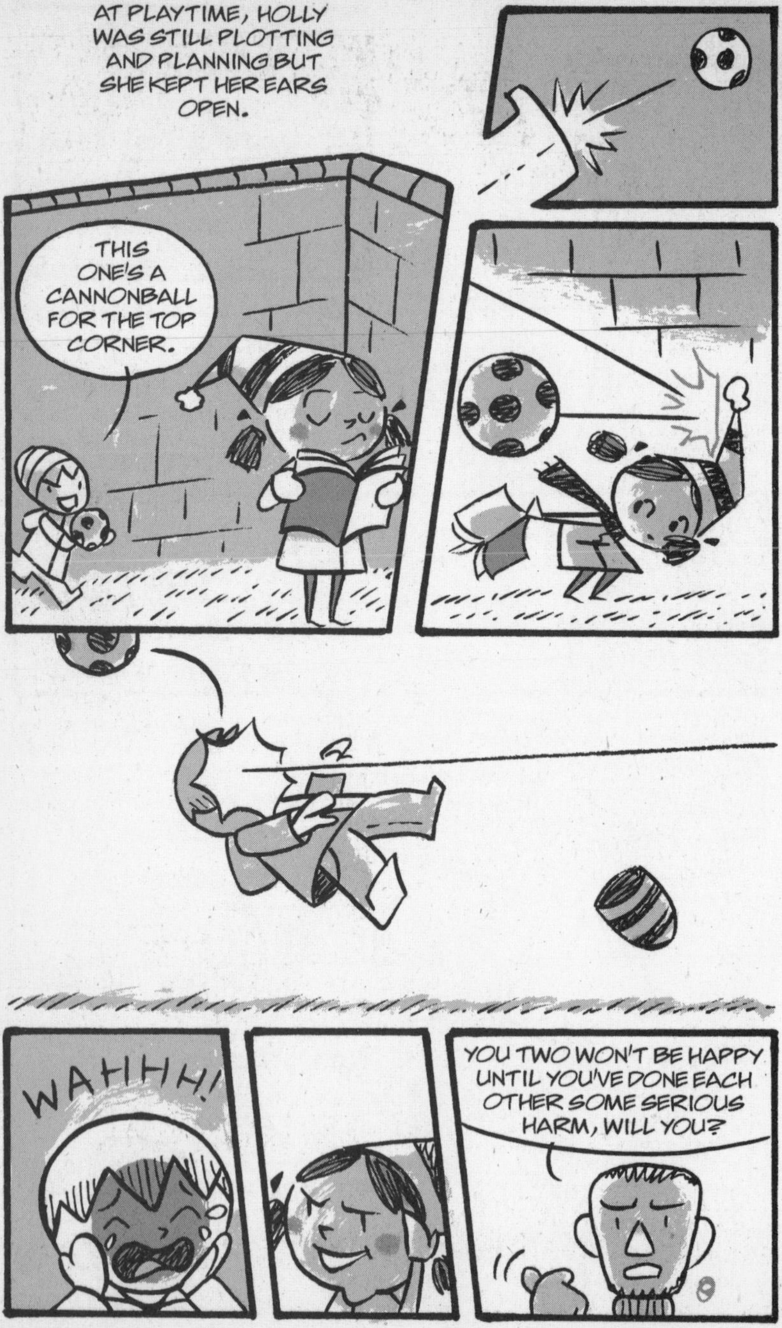
AT PLAYTIME, HOLLY WAS STILL PLOTTING AND PLANNING BUT SHE KEPT HER EARS OPEN.
THIS ONE'S A CANNONBALL FOR THE TOP CORNER.
WAHHH!
YOU TWO WON'T BE HAPPY UNTIL YOU'VE DONE EACH OTHER SOME SERIOUS HARM, WILL YOU?

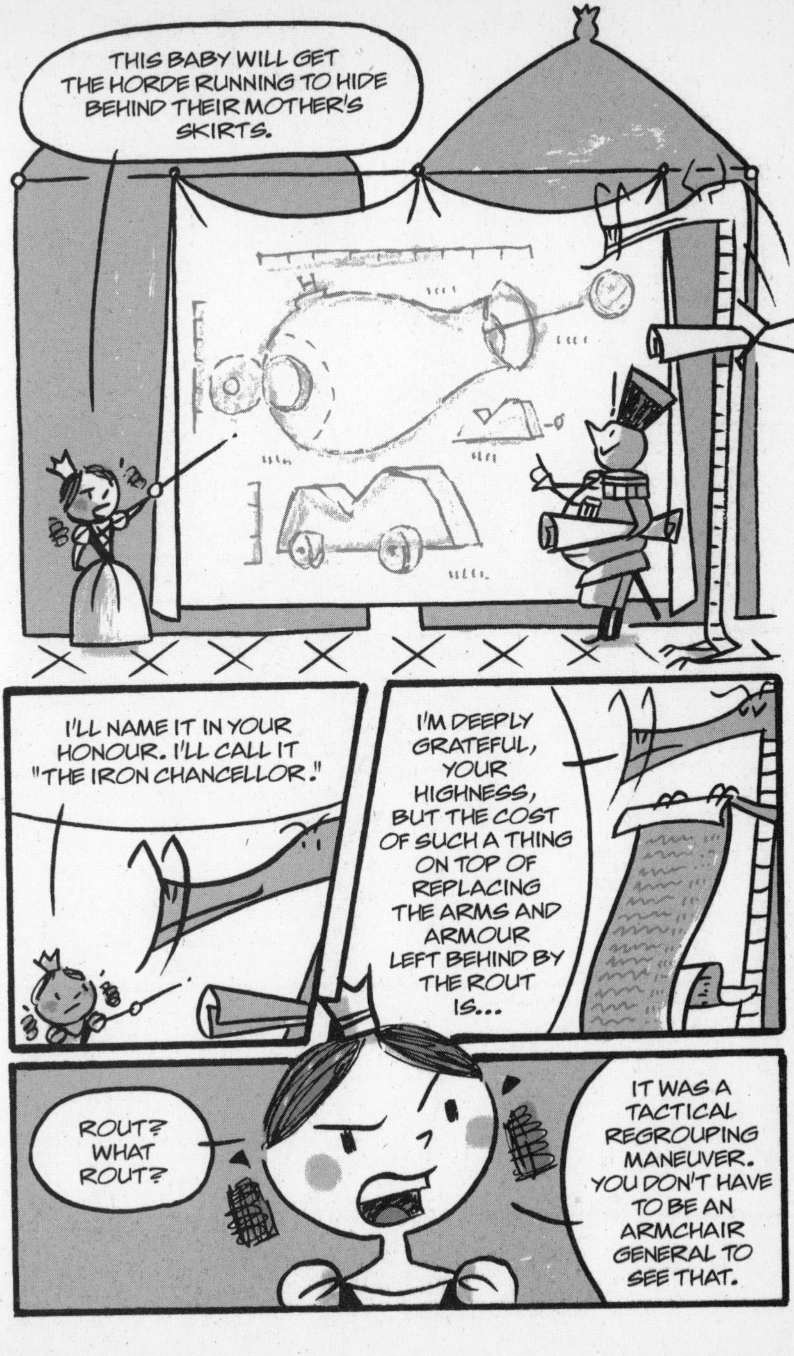
THIS BABY WILL GET THE HORDE RUNNING TO HIDE BEHIND THEIR MOTHER'S SKIRTS.
I'LL NAME IT IN YOUR HONOUR. I'LL CALL IT "THE IRON CHANCELLOR."
I'M DEEPLY GRATEFUL, YOUR HIGHNESS, BUT THE COST OF SUCH A THING ON TOP OF REPLACING THE ARMS AND ARMOUR LEFT BEHIND BY THE ROUT IS...
ROUT? WHAT ROUT?
IT WAS A TACTICAL REGROUPING MANEUVER. YOU DON'T HAVE TO BE AN ARMCHAIR GENERAL TO SEE THAT.

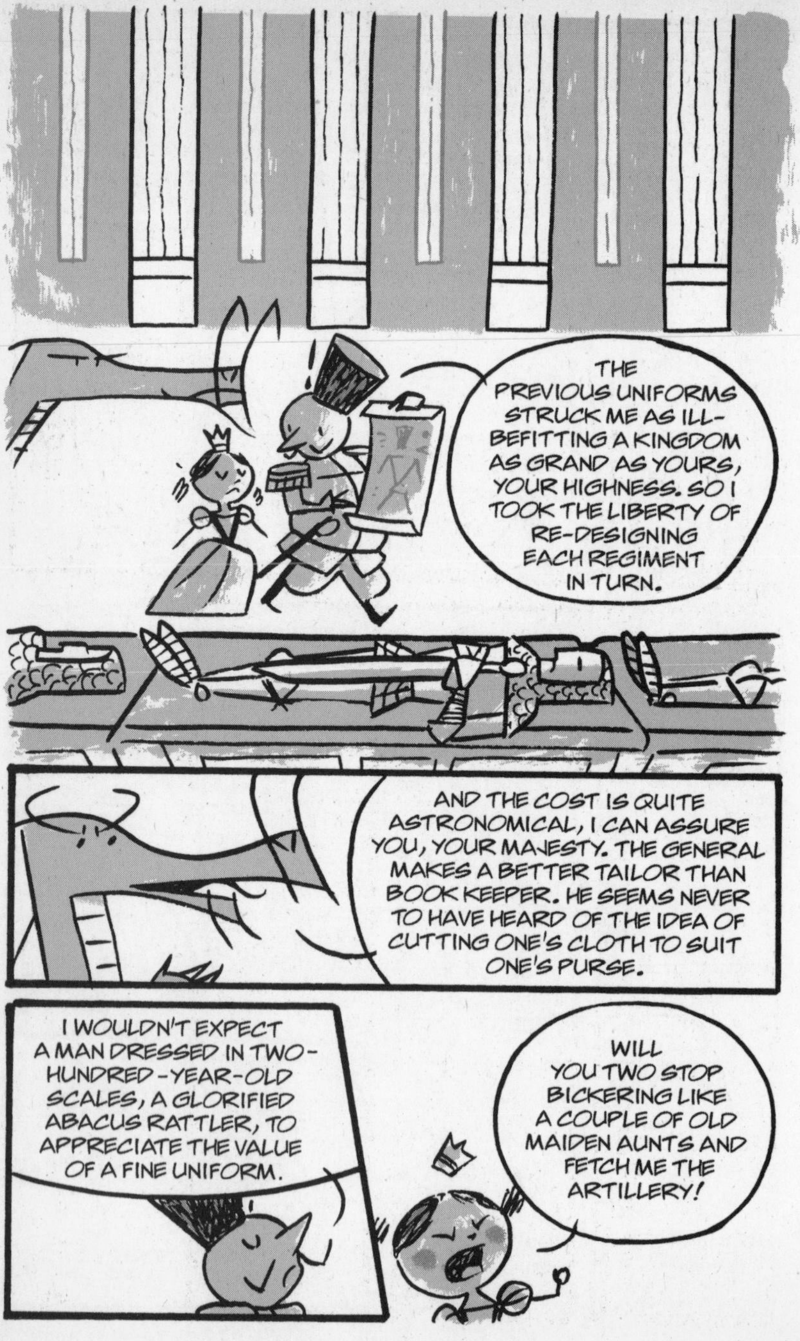
THE PREVIOUS UNIFORMS STRUCK ME AS ILL-BEFITTING A KINGDOM AS GRAND AS YOURS, YOUR HIGHNESS. SO I TOOK THE LIBERTY OF RE-DESIGNING EACH REGIMENT IN TURN.
AND THE COST IS QUITE ASTRONOMICAL, I CAN ASSURE YOU, YOUR MAJESTY. THE GENERAL MAKES A BETTER TAILOR THAN BOOK KEEPER. HE SEEMS NEVER TO HAVE HEARD OF THE IDEA OF CUTTING ONE'S CLOTH TO SUIT ONE'S PURSE.
I WOULDN'T EXPECT A MAN DRESSED IN TWO-HUNDRED-YEAR-OLD SCALES, A GLORIFIED ABACUS RATTLER, TO APPRECIATE THE VALUE OF A FINE UNIFORM.
WILL YOU TWO STOP BICKERING LIKE A COUPLE OF OLD MAIDEN AUNTS AND FETCH ME THE ARTILLERY!

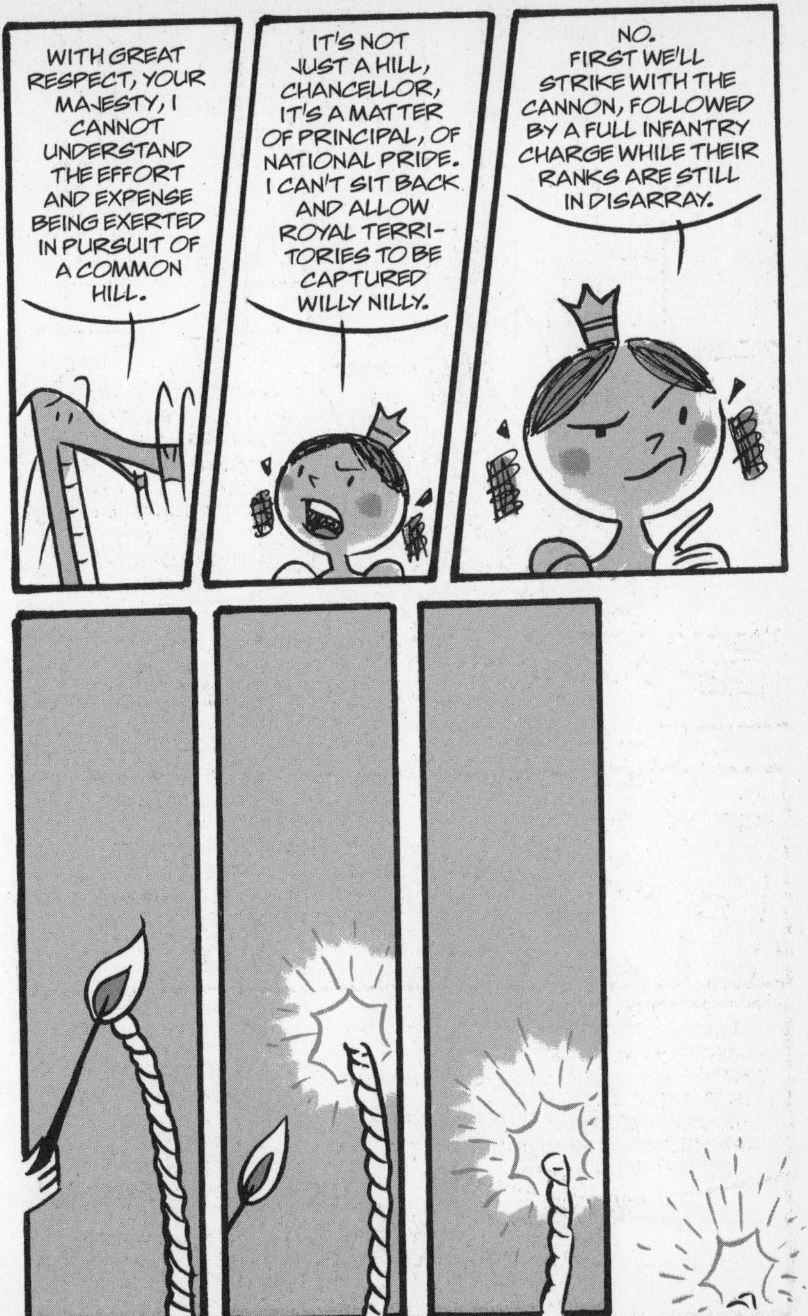
WITH GREAT RESPECT, YOUR MAJESTY, I CANNOT UNDERSTAND THE EFFORT AND EXPENSE BEING EXERTED IN PURSUIT OF A COMMON HILL.
IT'S NOT JUST A HILL, CHANCELLOR, IT'S A MATTER OF PRINCIPAL, OF NATIONAL PRIDE. I CAN'T SIT BACK AND ALLOW ROYAL TERRITORIES TO BE CAPTURED WILLY NILLY.
NO. FIRST WE'LL STRIKE WITH THE CANNON, FOLLOWED BY A FULL INFANTRY CHARGE WHILE THEIR RANKS ARE STILL IN DISARRAY.

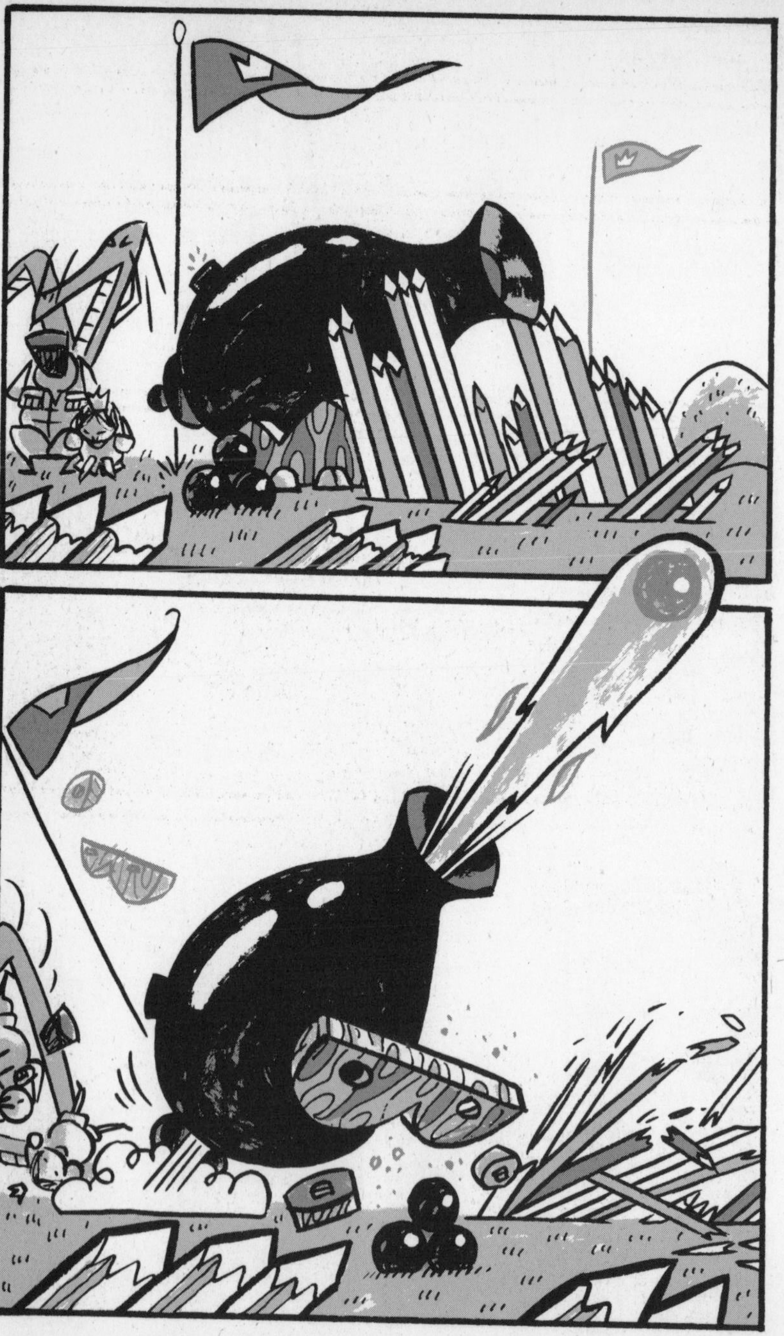

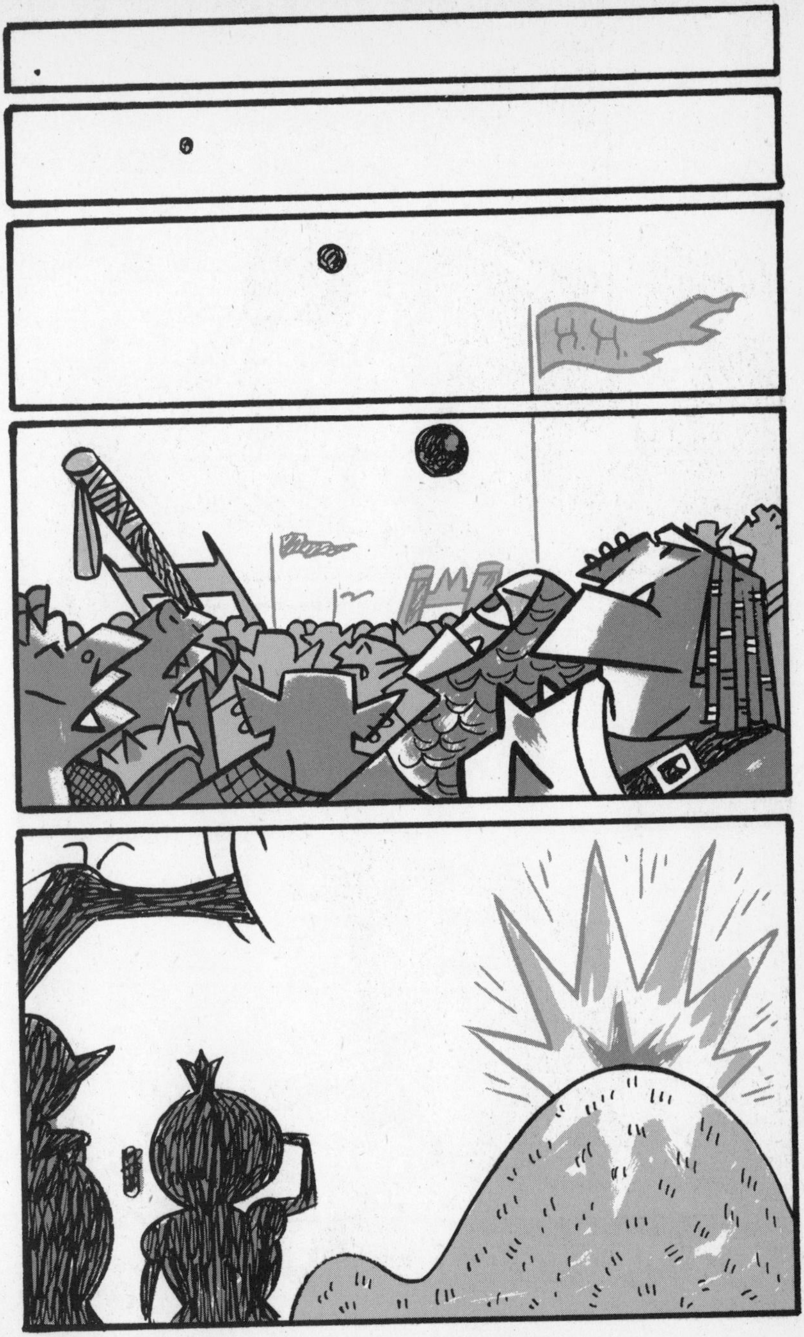
H.H.

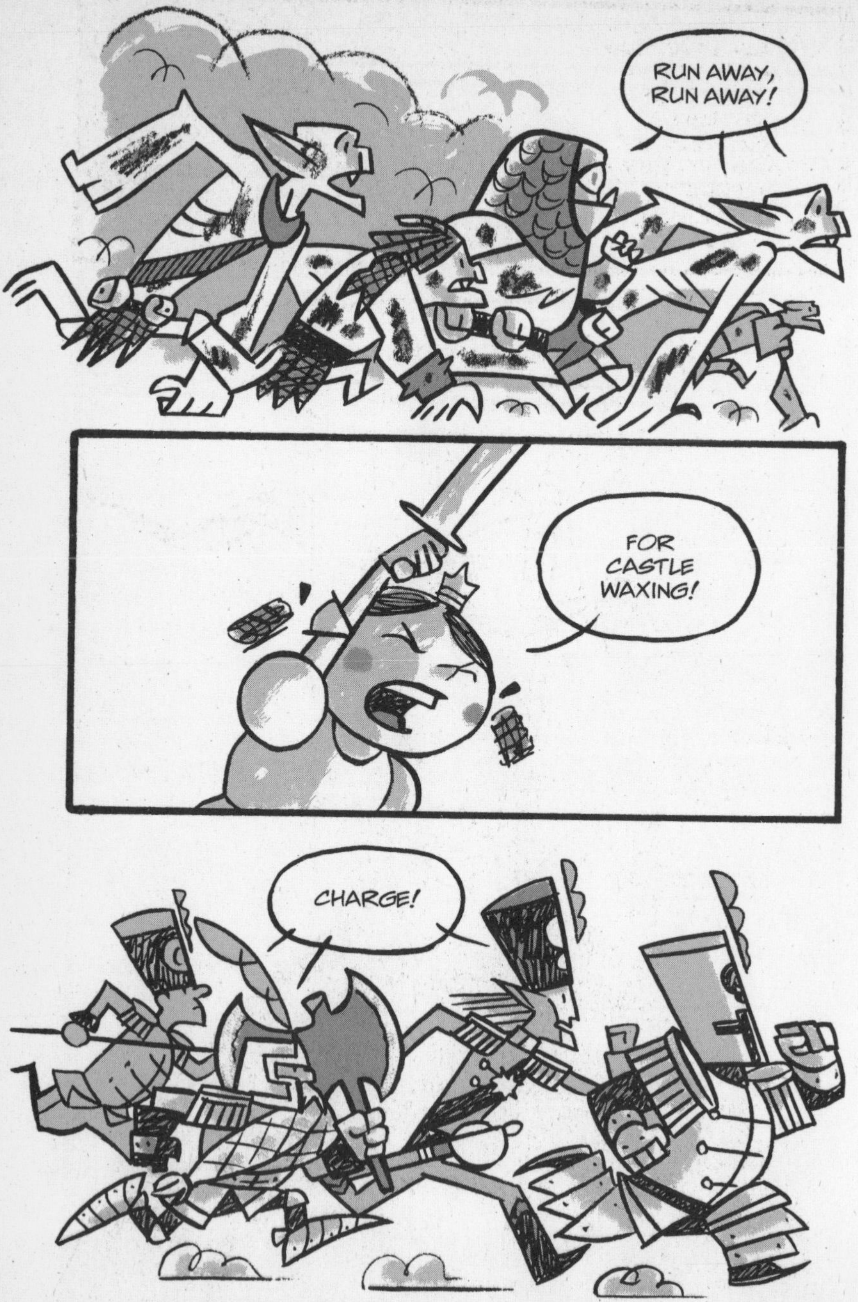
RUN AWAY, RUN AWAY!
FOR CASTLE WAXING!
CHARGE!

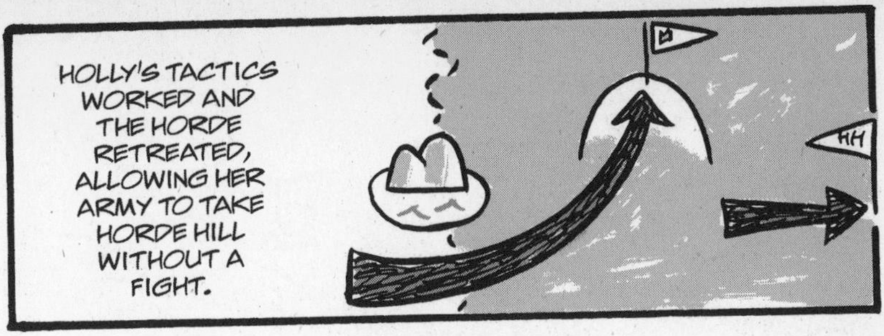
HOLLY'S TACTICS WORKED AND THE HORDE RETREATED, ALLOWING HER ARMY TO TAKE HORDE HILL WITHOUT A FIGHT.
HH

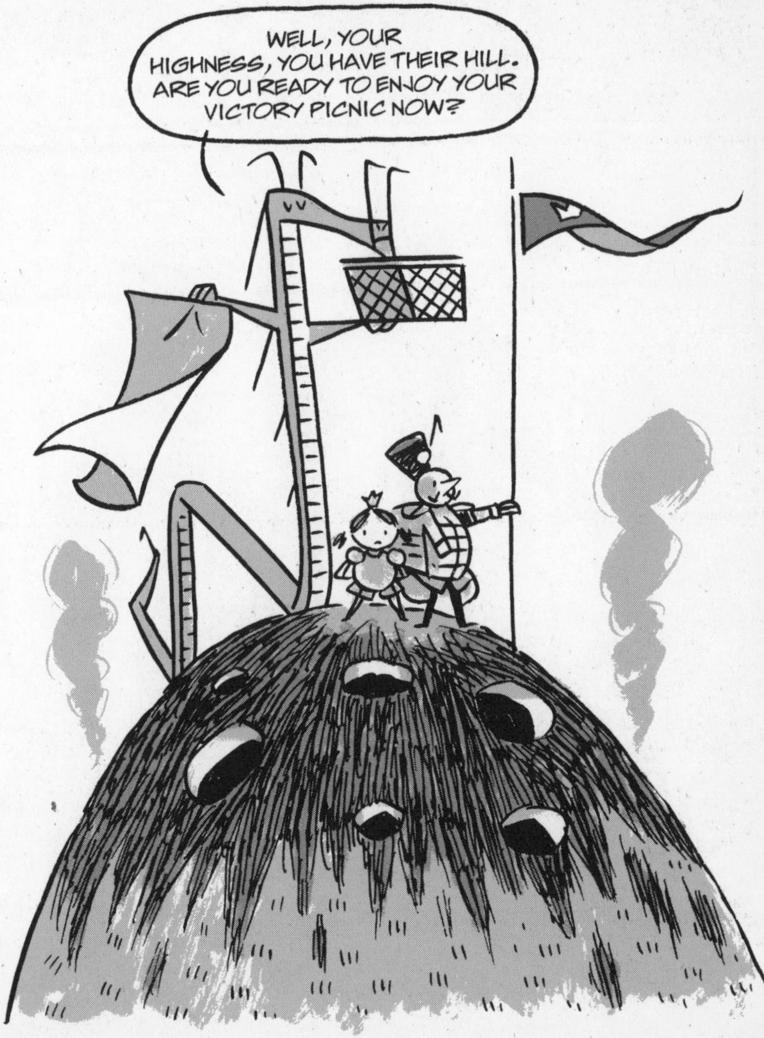
WELL, YOUR HIGHNESS, YOU HAVE THEIR HILL. ARE YOU READY TO ENJOY YOUR VICTORY PICNIC NOW?

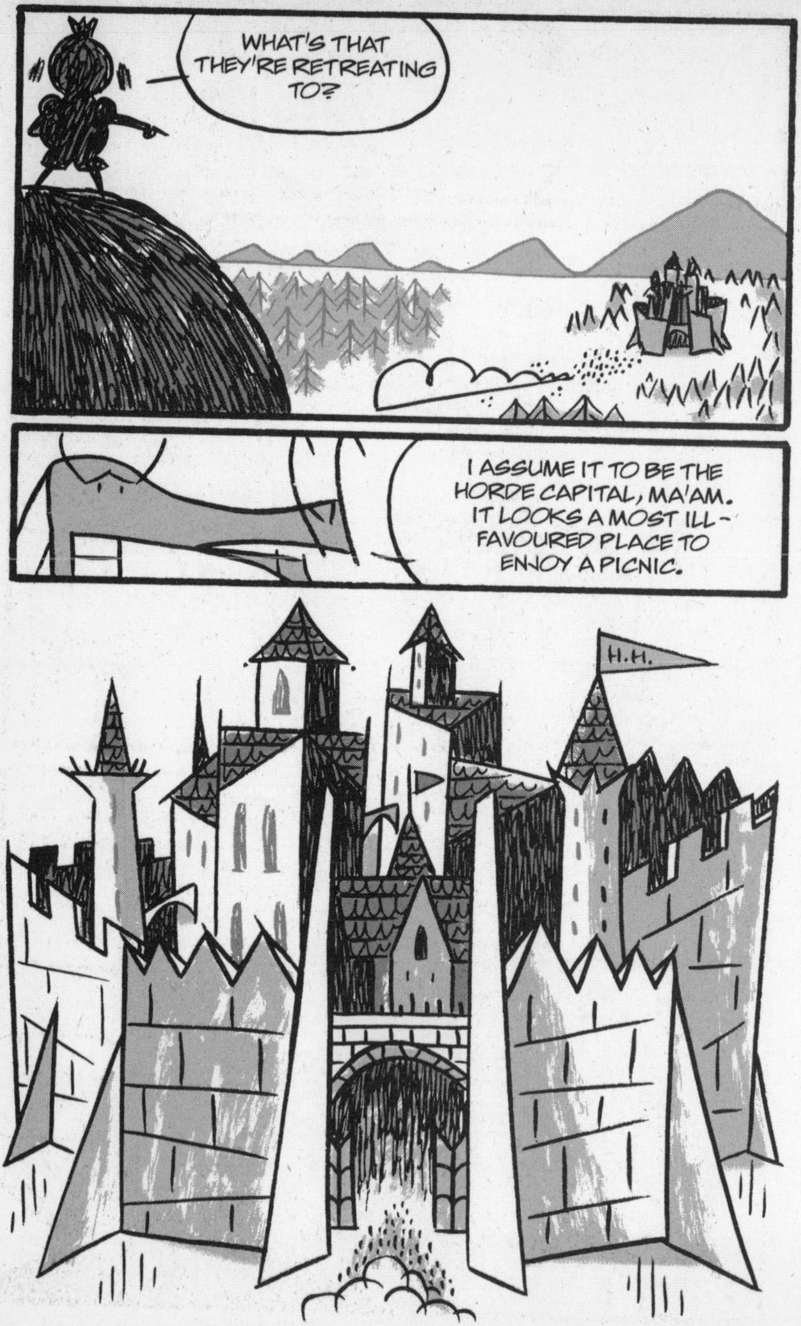
WHAT'S THAT THEY'RE RETREATING TO?
I ASSUME IT TO BE THE HORDE CAPITAL, MA'AM. IT LOOKS A MOST ILL-FAVOURED PLACE TO ENJOY A PICNIC.
H.H.

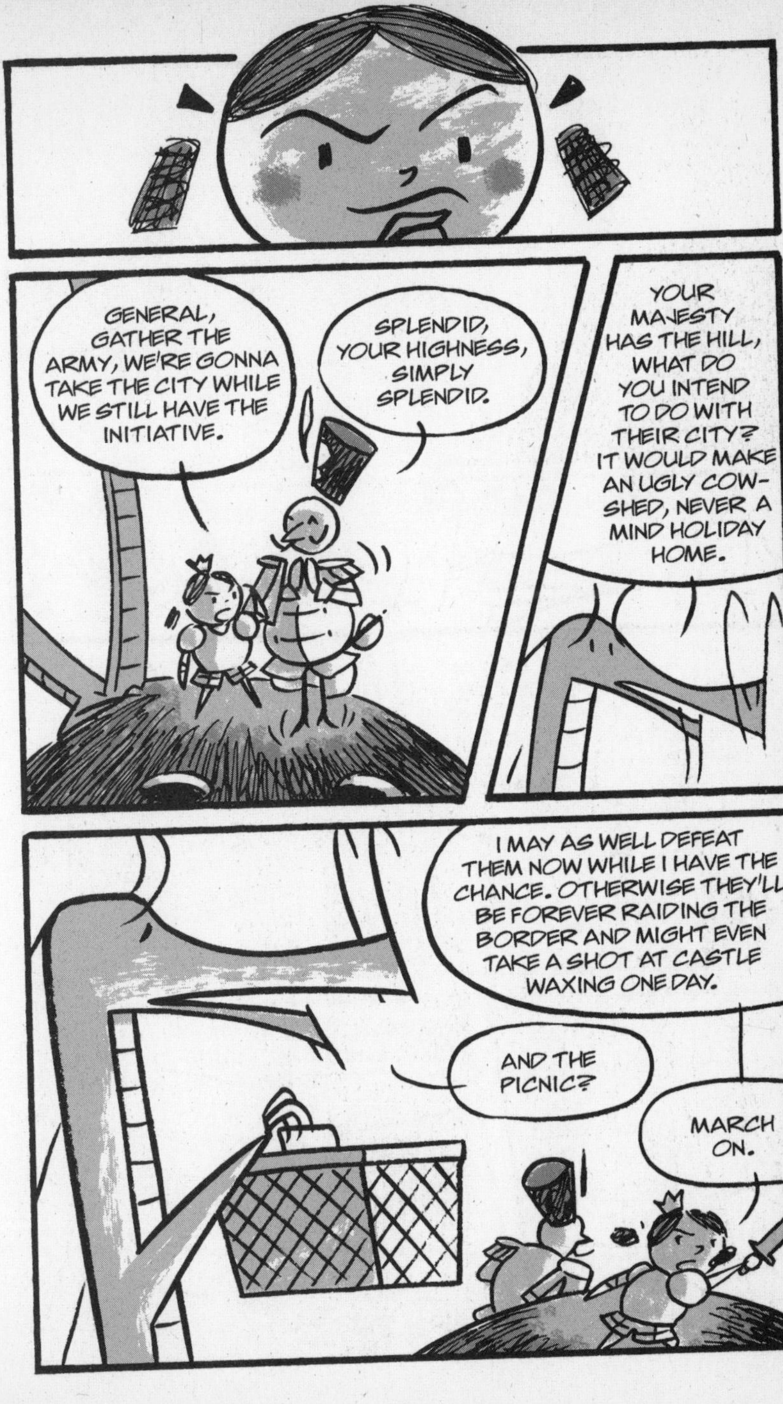
GENERAL, GATHER THE ARMY, WE'RE GONNA TAKE THE CITY WHILE WE STILL HAVE THE INITIATIVE.
SPLENDID, YOUR HIGHNESS, SIMPLY SPLENDID.
YOUR MAJESTY HAS THE HILL, WHAT DO YOU INTEND TO DO WITH THEIR CITY? IT WOULD MAKE AN UGLY COW-SHED, NEVER A MIND HOLIDAY HOME.
I MAY AS WELL DEFEAT THEM NOW WHILE I HAVE THE CHANCE. OTHERWISE THEY'LL BE FOREVER RAIDING THE BORDER AND MIGHT EVEN TAKE A SHOT AT CASTLE WAXING ONE DAY.
AND THE PICNIC?
MARCH ON.

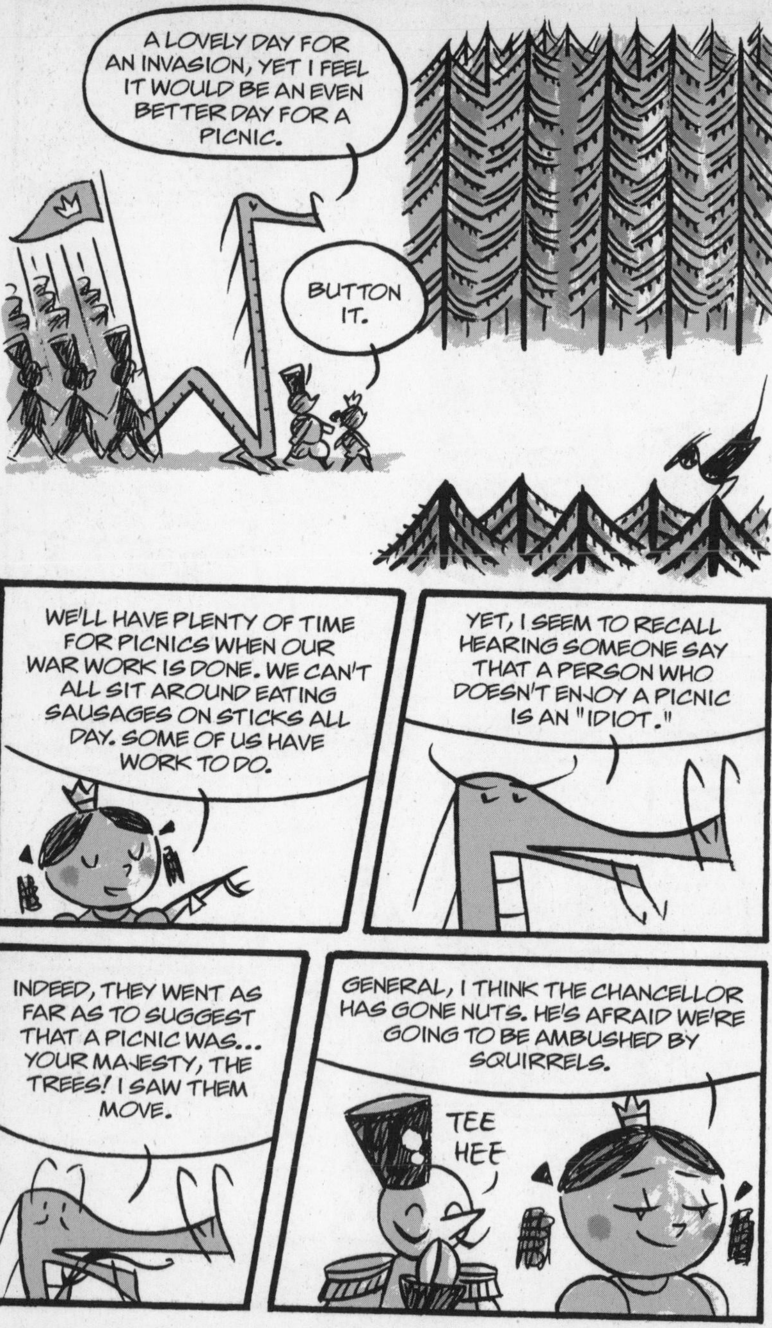
A LOVELY DAY FOR AN INVASION, YET I FEEL IT WOULD BE AN EVEN BETTER DAY FOR A PICNIC.
BUTTON IT.
WE'LL HAVE PLENTY OF TIME FOR PICNICS WHEN OUR WAR WORK IS DONE. WE CAN'T ALL SIT AROUND EATING SAUSAGES ON STICKS ALL DAY. SOME OF US HAVE WORK TO DO.
YET, I SEEM TO RECALL HEARING SOMEONE SAY THAT A PERSON WHO DOESN'T ENJOY A PICNIC IS AN "IDIOT."
INDEED, THEY WENT AS FAR AS TO SUGGEST THAT A PICNIC WAS... YOUR MAJESTY, THE TREES! I SAW THEM MOVE.
GENERAL, I THINK THE CHANCELLOR HAS GONE NUTS. HE'S AFRAID WE'RE GOING TO BE AMBUSHED BY SQUIRRELS.
TEE HEE

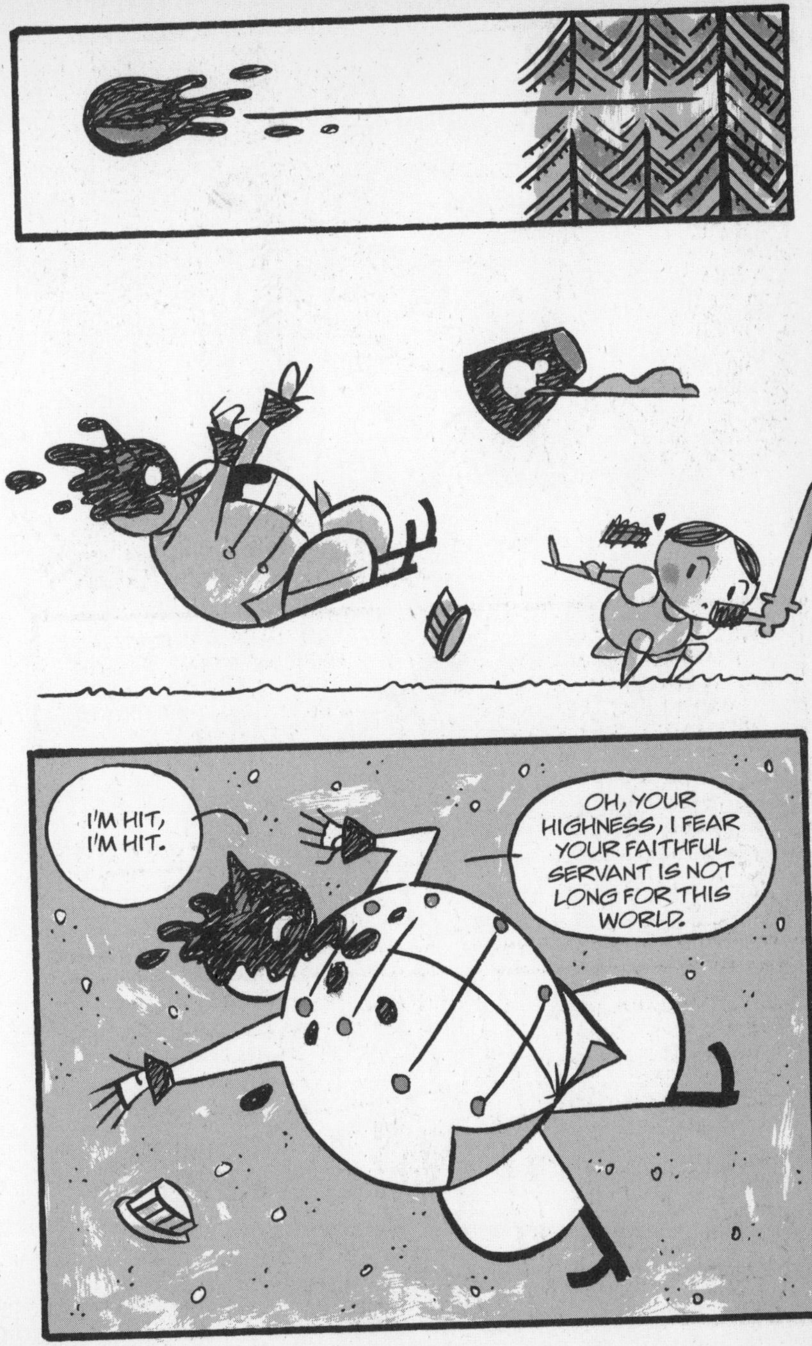
I'M HIT, I'M HIT.
OH, YOUR HIGHNESS, I FEAR YOUR FAITHFUL SERVANT IS NOT LONG FOR THIS WORLD.

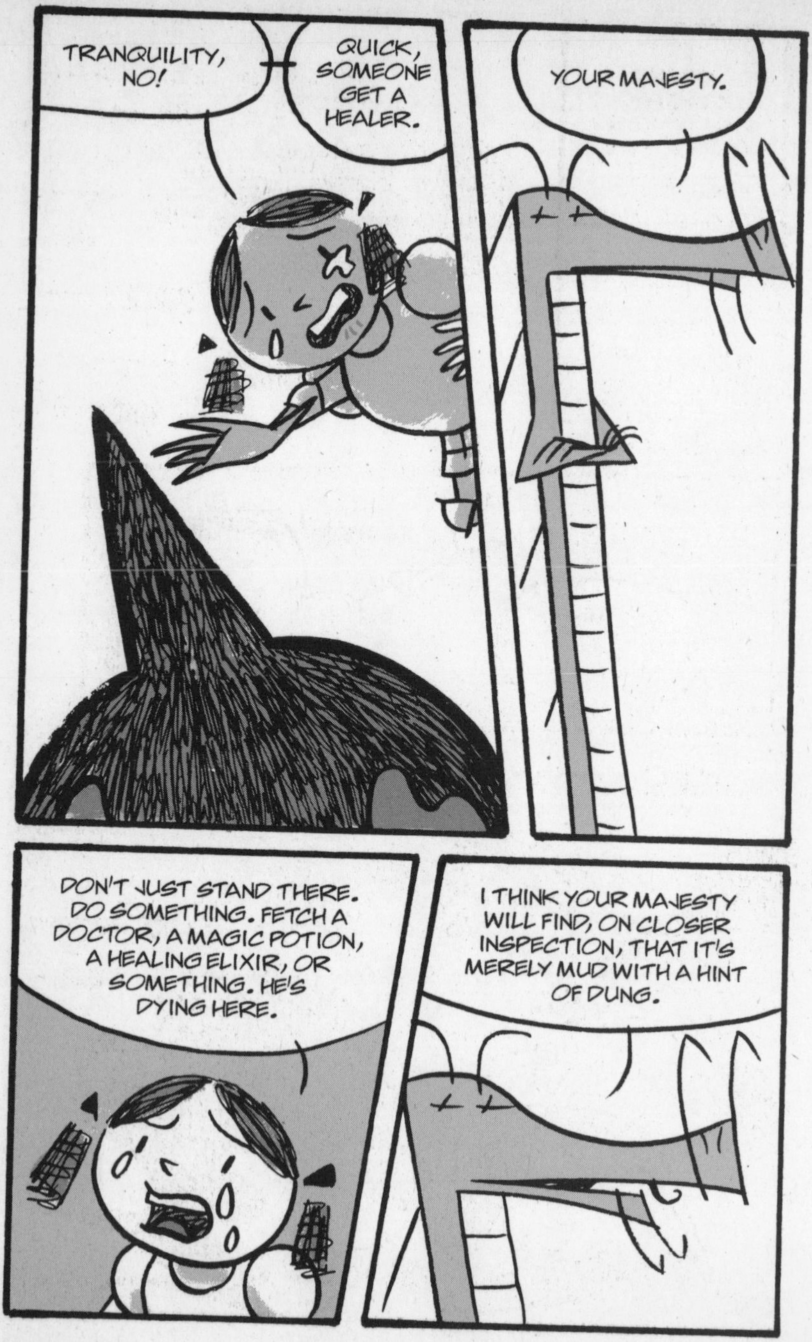
TRANQUILITY, NO!
QUICK, SOMEONE GET A HEALER.
YOUR MAJESTY.
DON'T JUST STAND THERE. DO SOMETHING. FETCH A DOCTOR, A MAGIC POTION, A HEALING ELIXIR, OR SOMETHING. HE'S DYING HERE.
I THINK YOUR MAJESTY WILL FIND, ON CLOSER INSPECTION, THAT IT'S MERELY MUD WITH A HINT OF DUNG.

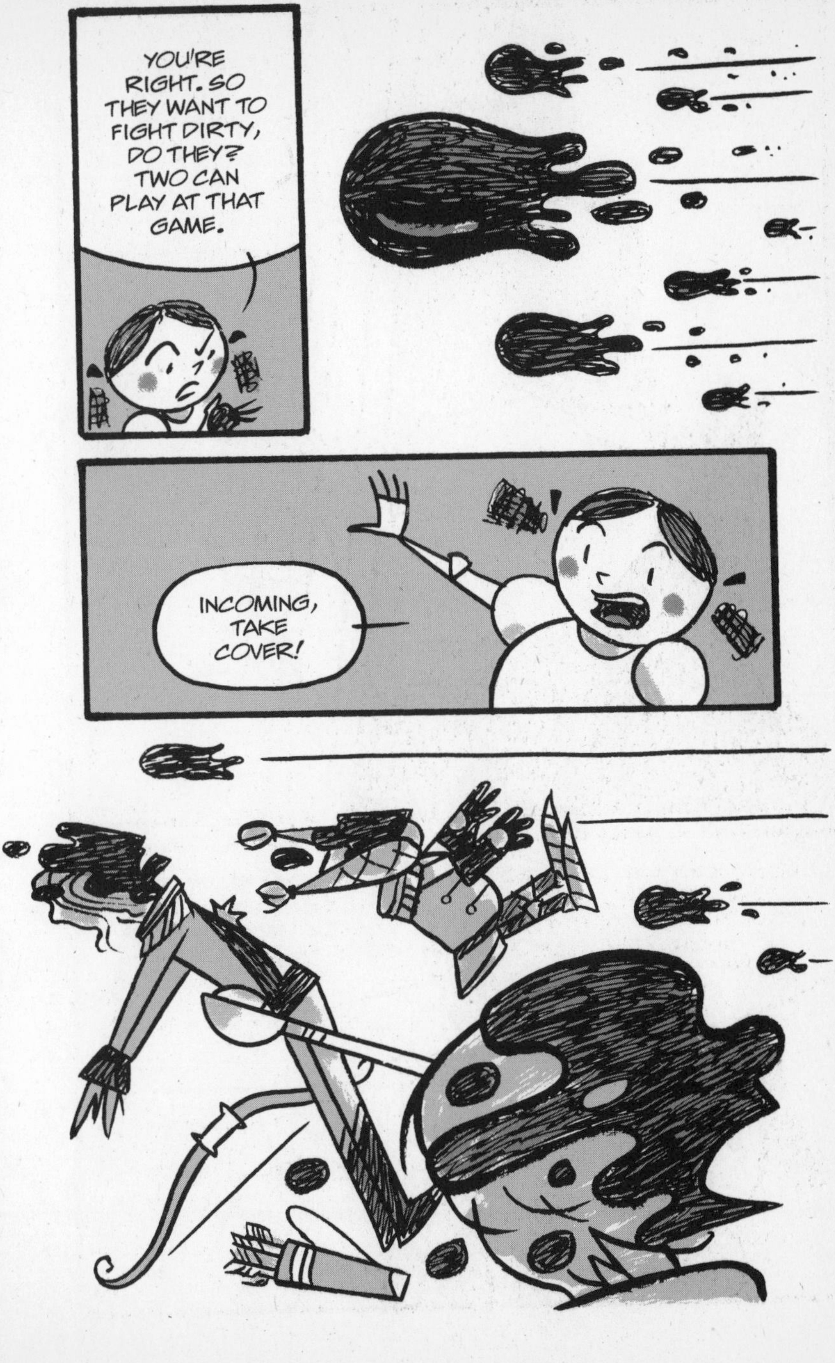
YOU'RE RIGHT. SO THEY WANT TO FIGHT DIRTY, DO THEY? TWO CAN PLAY AT THAT GAME.
INCOMING, TAKE COVER!

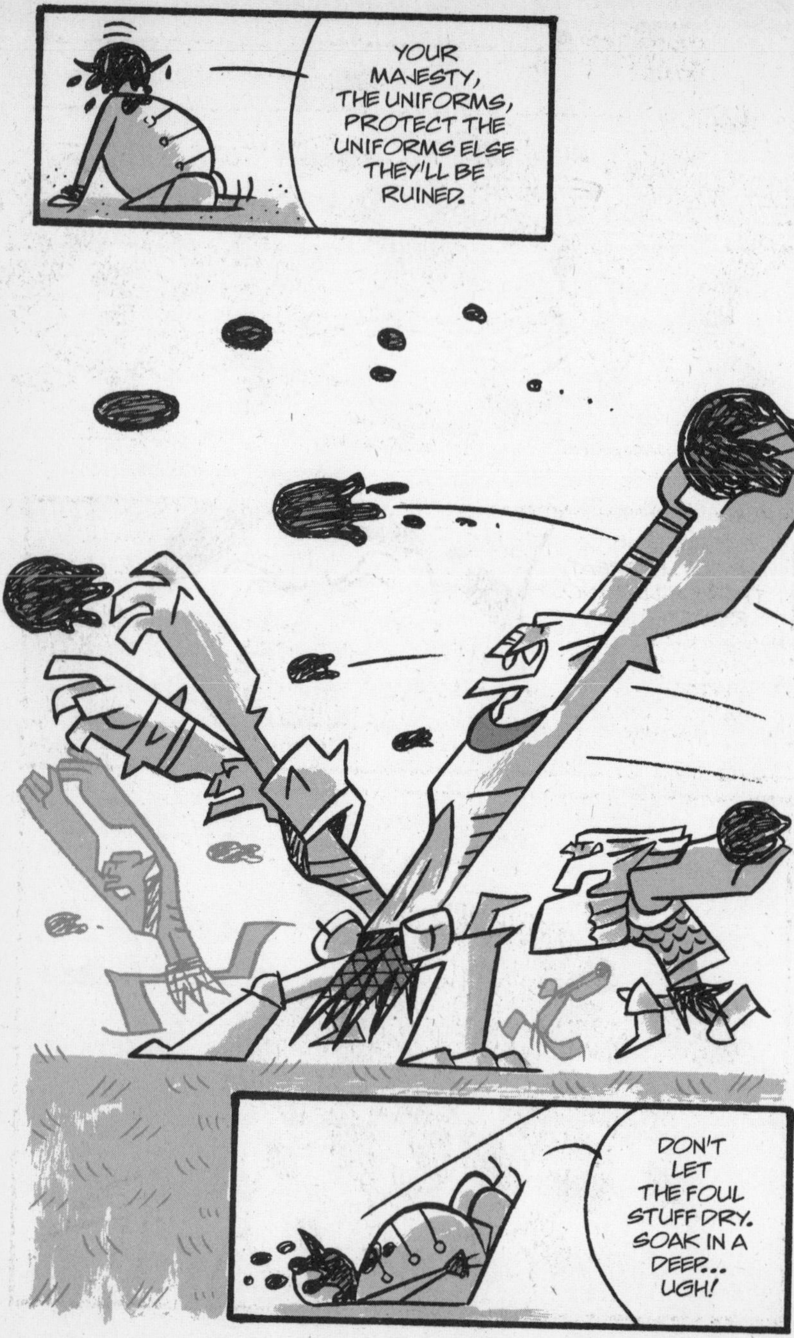
YOUR MAJESTY, THE UNIFORMS, PROTECT THE UNIFORMS ELSE THEY'LL BE RUINED.
DON'T LET THE FOUL STUFF DRY. SOAK IN A DEEP... UGH!

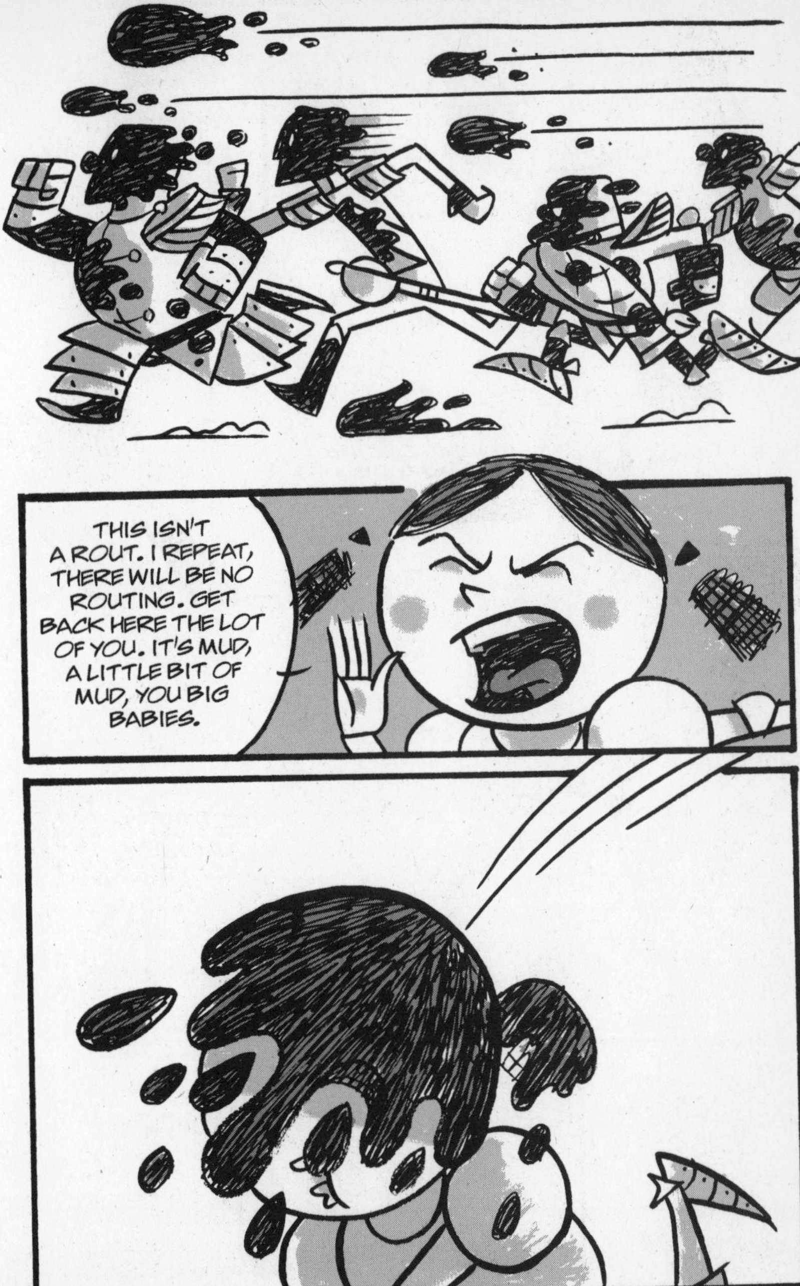
THIS ISN'T A ROUT. I REPEAT, THERE WILL BE NO ROUTING. GET BACK HERE THE LOT OF YOU. IT'S MUD, A LITTLE BIT OF MUD, YOU BIG BABIES.

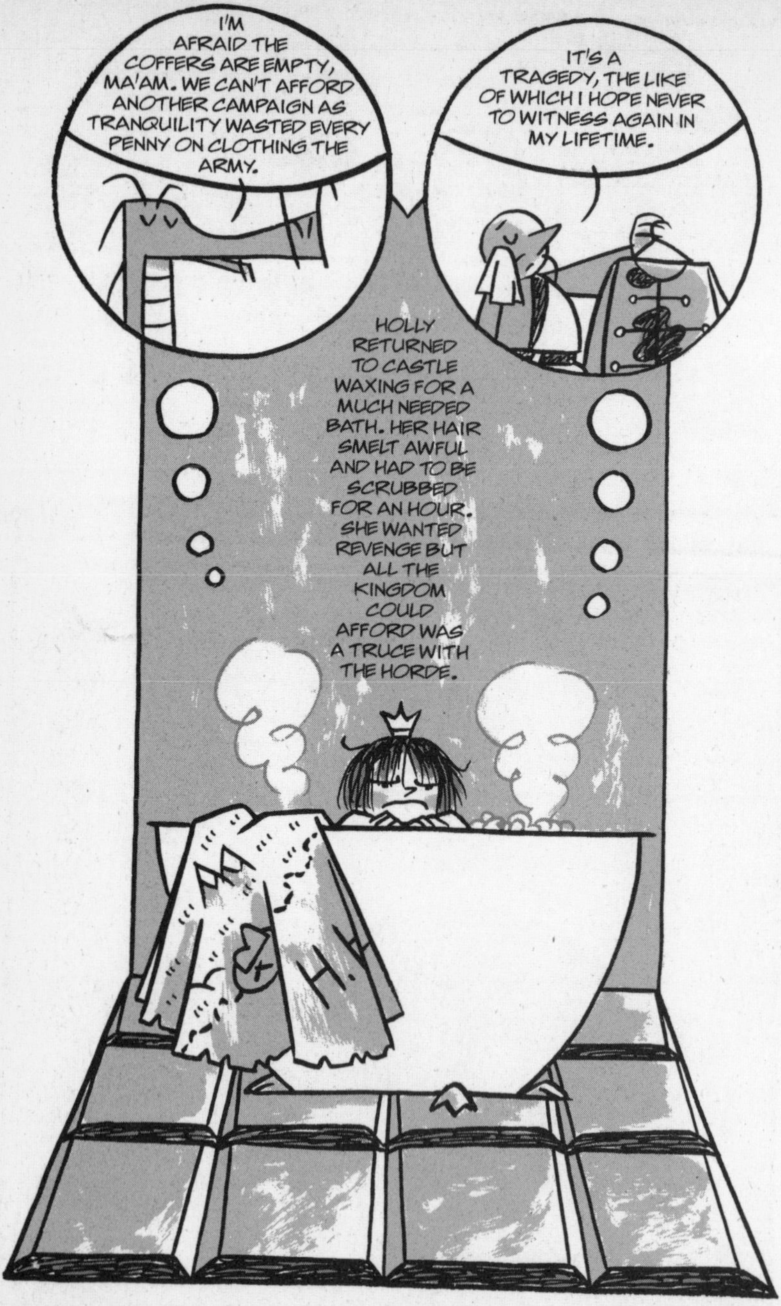
I'M AFRAID THE COFFERS ARE EMPTY, MA'AM. WE CAN'T AFFORD ANOTHER CAMPAIGN AS TRANQUILITY WASTED EVERY PENNY ON CLOTHING THE ARMY.
IT'S A TRAGEDY, THE LIKE OF WHICH I HOPE NEVER TO WITNESS AGAIN IN MY LIFETIME.
HOLLY RETURNED TO CASTLE WAXING FOR A MUCH NEEDED BATH. HER HAIR SMELT AWFUL AND HAD TO BE SCRUBBED FOR AN HOUR. SHE WANTED REVENGE BUT ALL THE KINGDOM COULD AFFORD WAS A TRUCE WITH THE HORDE.

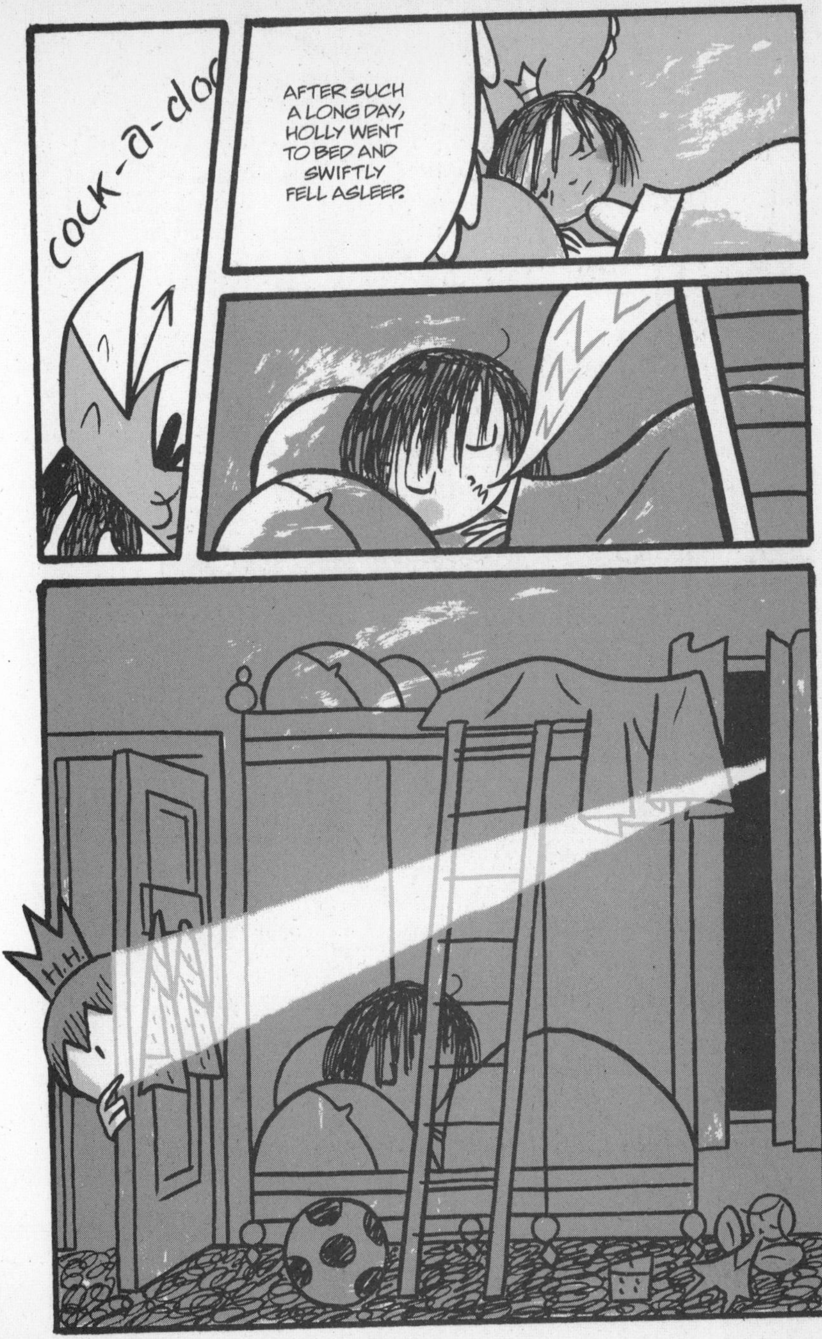

cock-a-doo
AFTER SUCH A LONG DAY, HOLLY WENT TO BED AND SWIFTLY FELL ASLEEP.
H.H.

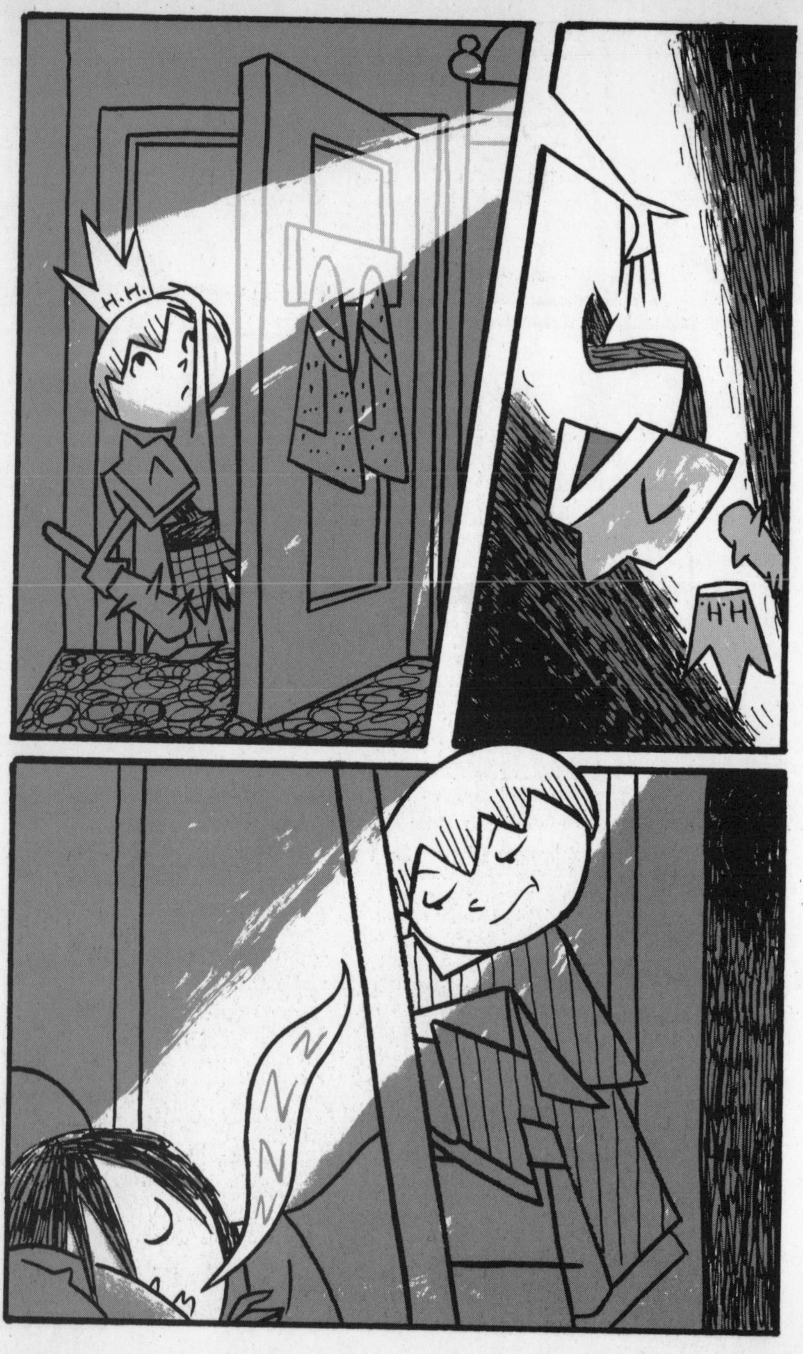
H.H.
H·H

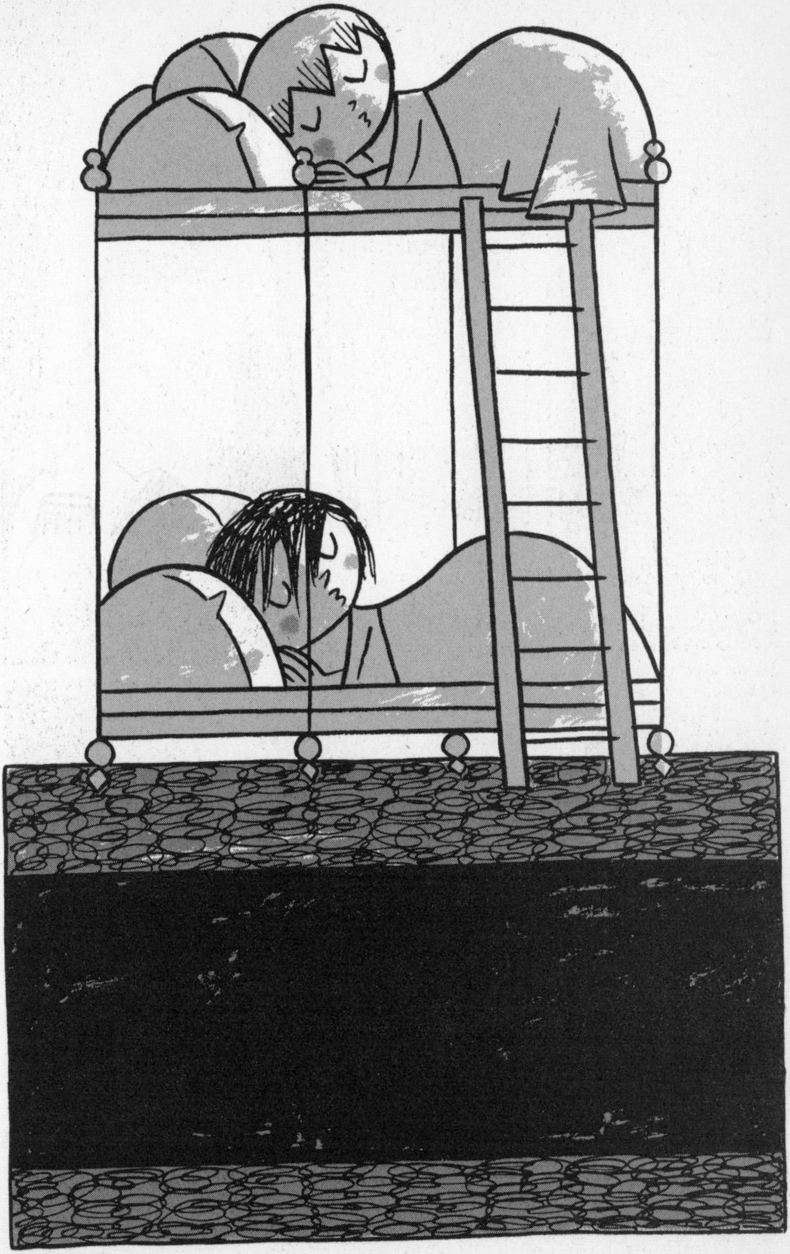

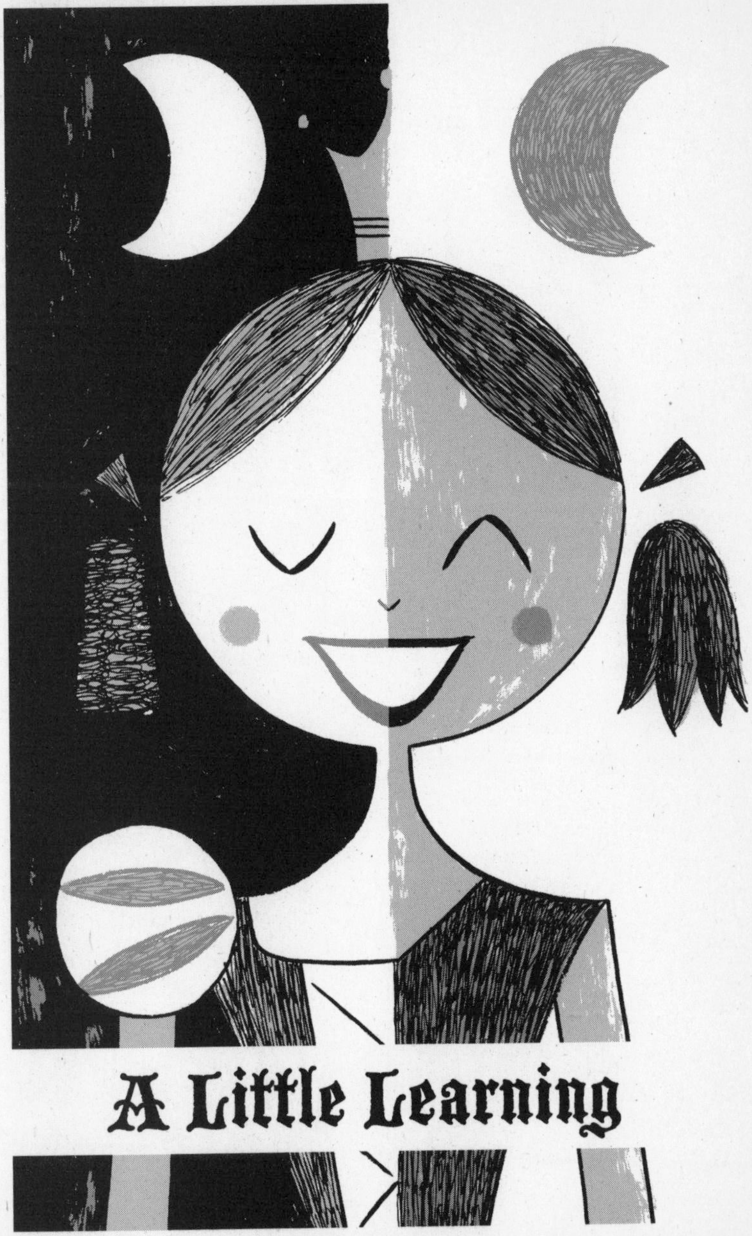
A Little Learning

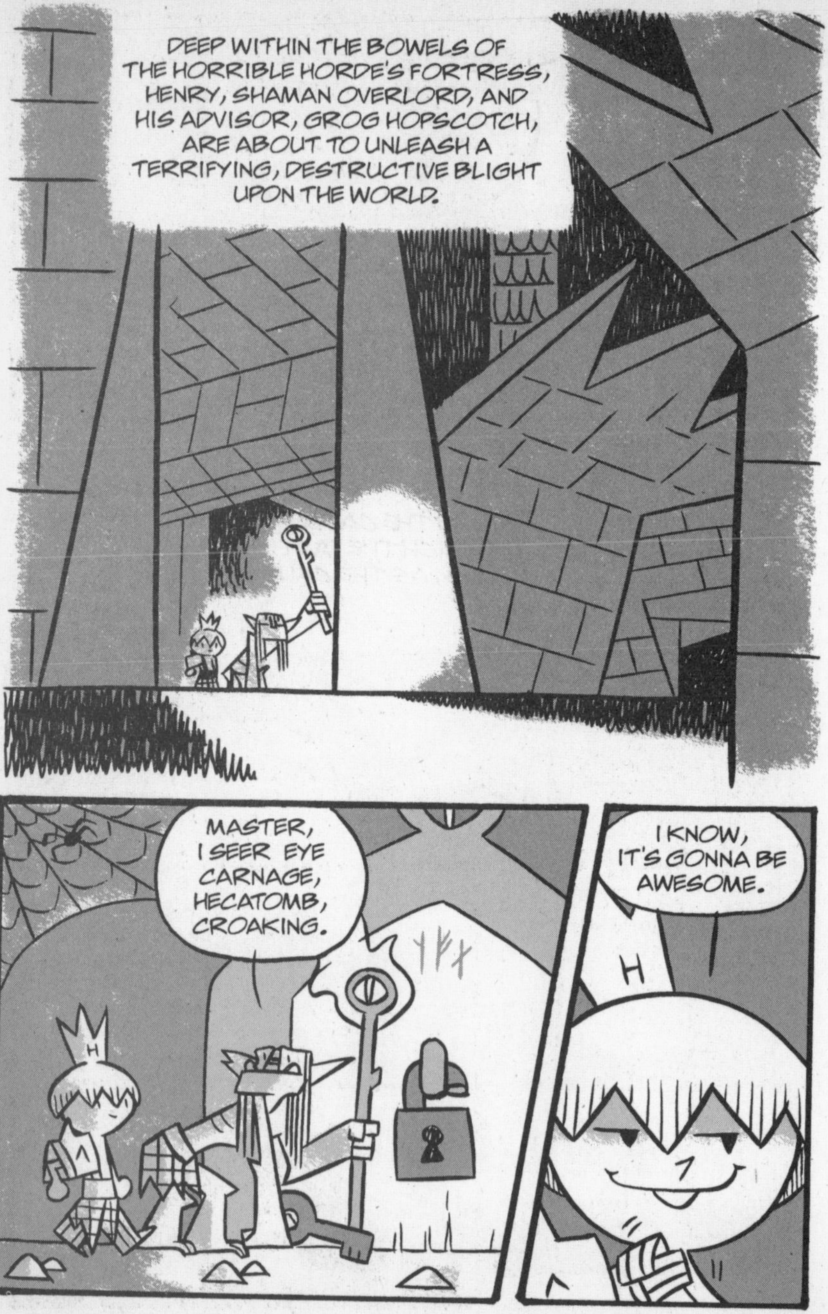
DEEP WITHIN THE BOWELS OF THE HORRIBLE HORDE'S FORTRESS, HENRY, SHAMAN OVERLORD, AND HIS ADVISOR, GROG HOPSCOTCH, ARE ABOUT TO UNLEASH A TERRIFYING, DESTRUCTIVE BLIGHT UPON THE WORLD.
MASTER, I SEER EYE CARNAGE, HECATOMB, CROAKING.
I KNOW, IT'S GONNA BE AWESOME.

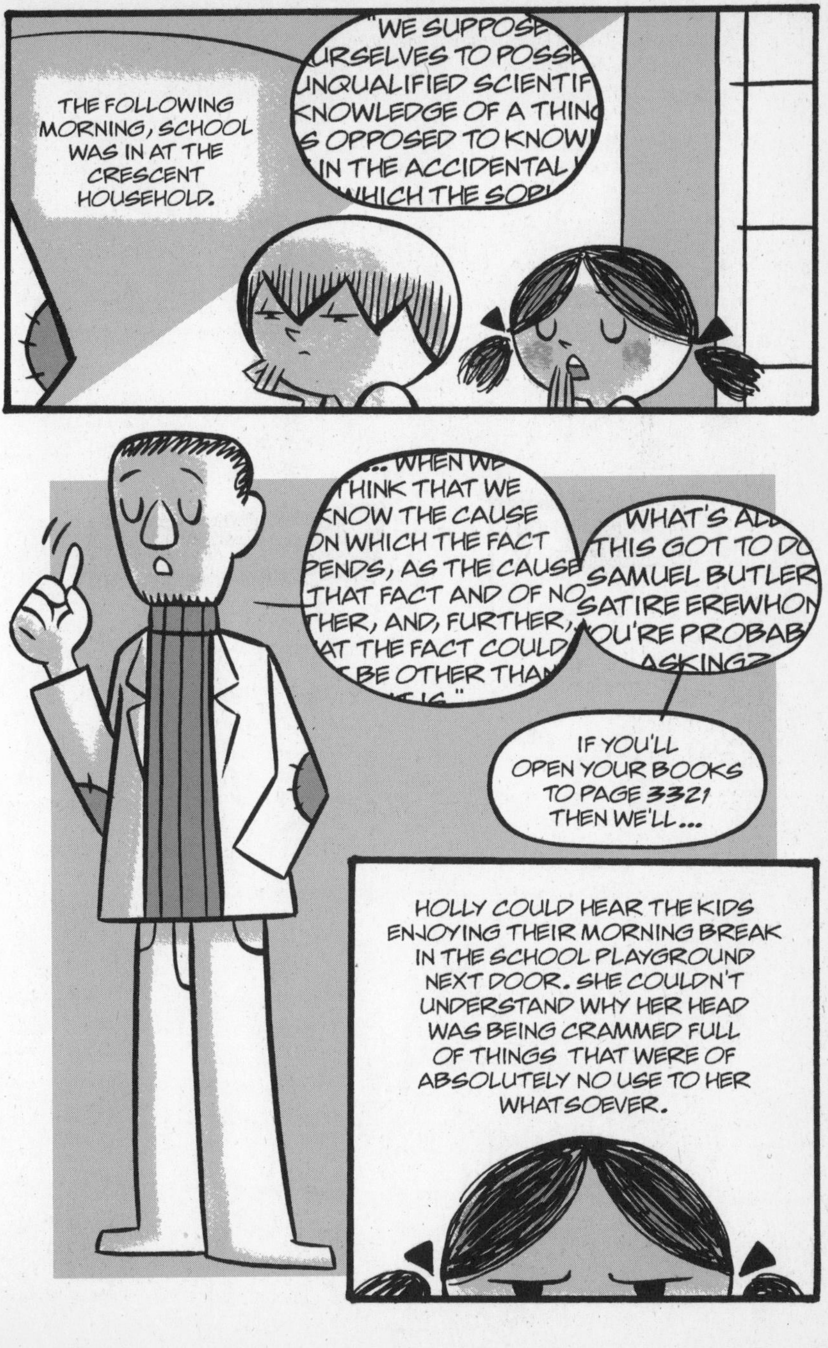
THE FOLLOWING MORNING, SCHOOL WAS IN AT THE CRESCENT HOUSEHOLD.
"WE SUPPOSE URSELVES TO POSSE UNQUALIFIED SCIENTIF KNOWLEDGE OF A THIN S OPPOSED TO KNOW IN THE ACCIDENTAL WHICH THE SOP
... WHEN W THINK THAT WE KNOW THE CAUSE ON WHICH THE FACT PENDS, AS THE CAUSE THAT FACT AND OF NO THER, AND, FURTHER, AT THE FACT COULD BE OTHER THAN
WHAT'S AL THIS GOT TO D SAMUEL BUTLER SATIRE EREWHON OU'RE PROBAB ASKING?
IF YOU'LL OPEN YOUR BOOKS TO PAGE 3321 THEN WE'LL...
HOLLY COULD HEAR THE KIDS ENJOYING THEIR MORNING BREAK IN THE SCHOOL PLAYGROUND NEXT DOOR. SHE COULDN'T UNDERSTAND WHY HER HEAD WAS BEING CRAMMED FULL OF THINGS THAT WERE OF ABSOLUTELY NO USE TO HER WHATSOEVER.

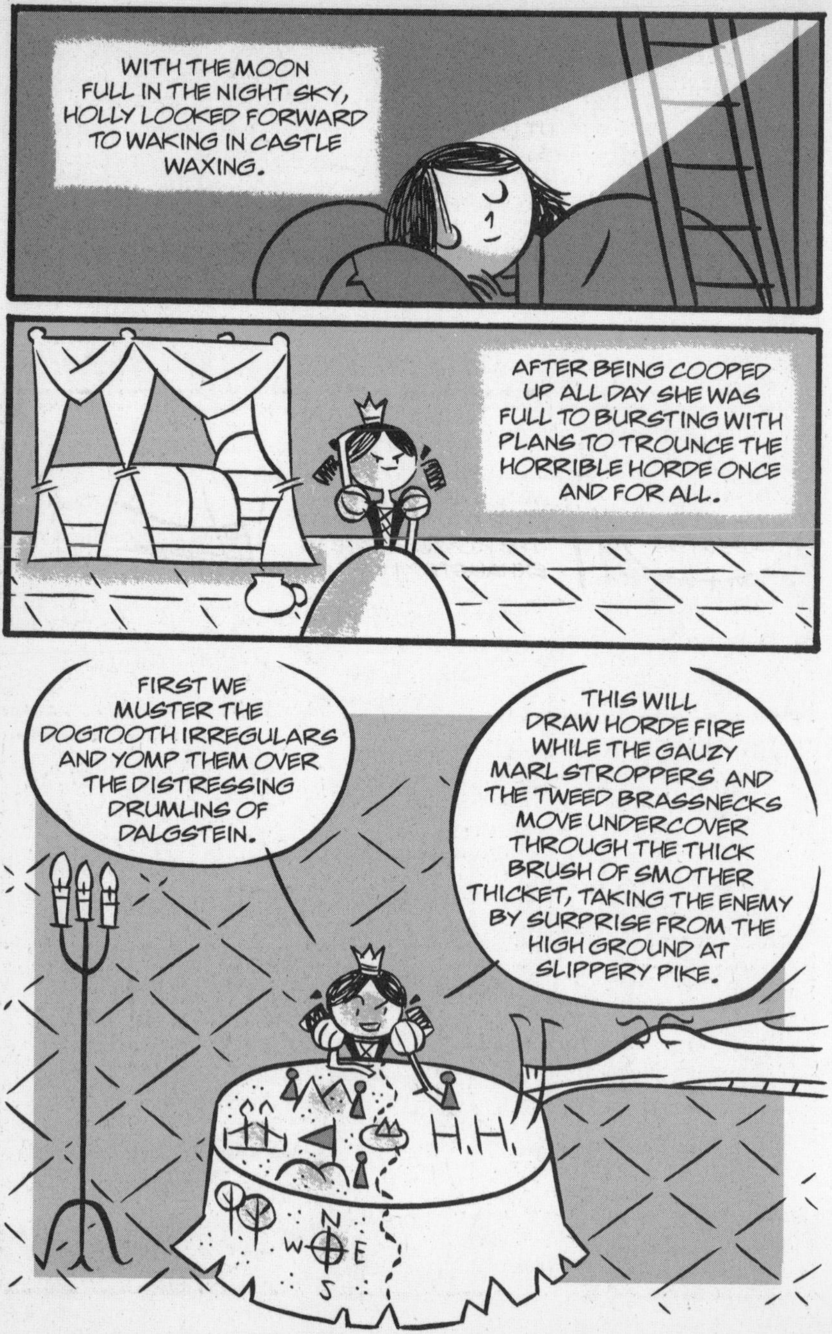

WITH THE MOON FULL IN THE NIGHT SKY, HOLLY LOOKED FORWARD TO WAKING IN CASTLE WAXING.
AFTER BEING COOPED UP ALL DAY SHE WAS FULL TO BURSTING WITH PLANS TO TROUNCE THE HORRIBLE HORDE ONCE AND FOR ALL.
FIRST WE MUSTER THE DOGTOOTH IRREGULARS AND YOMP THEM OVER THE DISTRESSING DRUMLINS OF DALGSTEIN.
THIS WILL DRAW HORDE FIRE WHILE THE GAUZY MARL STROPPERS AND THE TWEED BRASSNECKS MOVE UNDERCOVER THROUGH THE THICK BRUSH OF SMOTHER THICKET, TAKING THE ENEMY BY SURPRISE FROM THE HIGH GROUND AT SLIPPERY PIKE.
H.H.
N
W
E
S

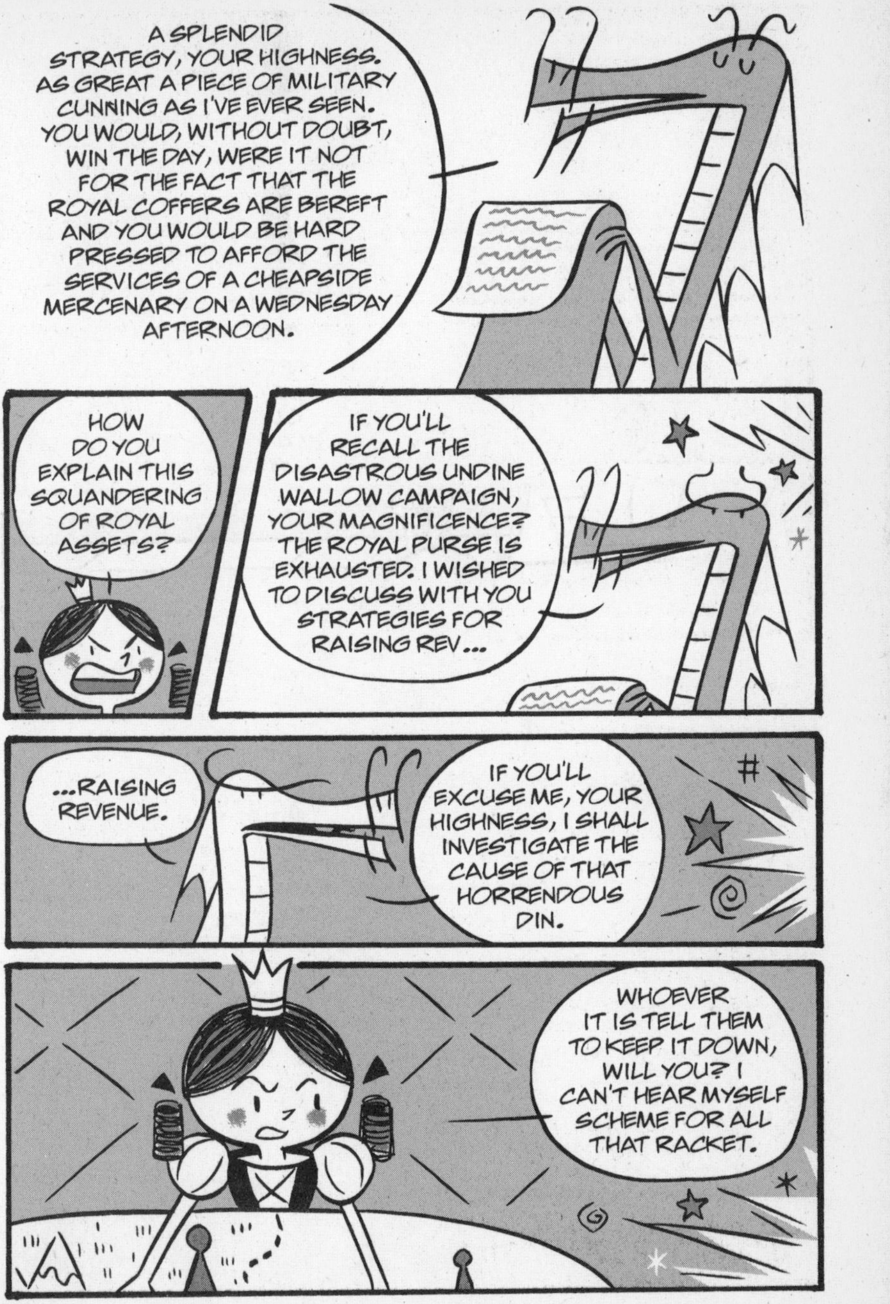
A SPLENDID STRATEGY, YOUR HIGHNESS. AS GREAT A PIECE OF MILITARY CUNNING AS I'VE EVER SEEN. YOU WOULD, WITHOUT DOUBT, WIN THE DAY, WERE IT NOT FOR THE FACT THAT THE ROYAL COFFERS ARE BEREFT AND YOU WOULD BE HARD PRESSED TO AFFORD THE SERVICES OF A CHEAPSIDE MERCENARY ON A WEDNESDAY AFTERNOON.
HOW DO YOU EXPLAIN THIS SQUANDERING OF ROYAL ASSETS?
IF YOU'LL RECALL THE DISASTROUS UNDINE WALLOW CAMPAIGN, YOUR MAGNIFICENCE? THE ROYAL PURSE IS EXHAUSTED. I WISHED TO DISCUSS WITH YOU STRATEGIES FOR RAISING REV...
...RAISING REVENUE.
IF YOU'LL EXCUSE ME, YOUR HIGHNESS, I SHALL INVESTIGATE THE CAUSE OF THAT HORRENDOUS DIN.
WHOEVER IT IS TELL THEM TO KEEP IT DOWN, WILL YOU? I CAN'T HEAR MYSELF SCHEME FOR ALL THAT RACKET.

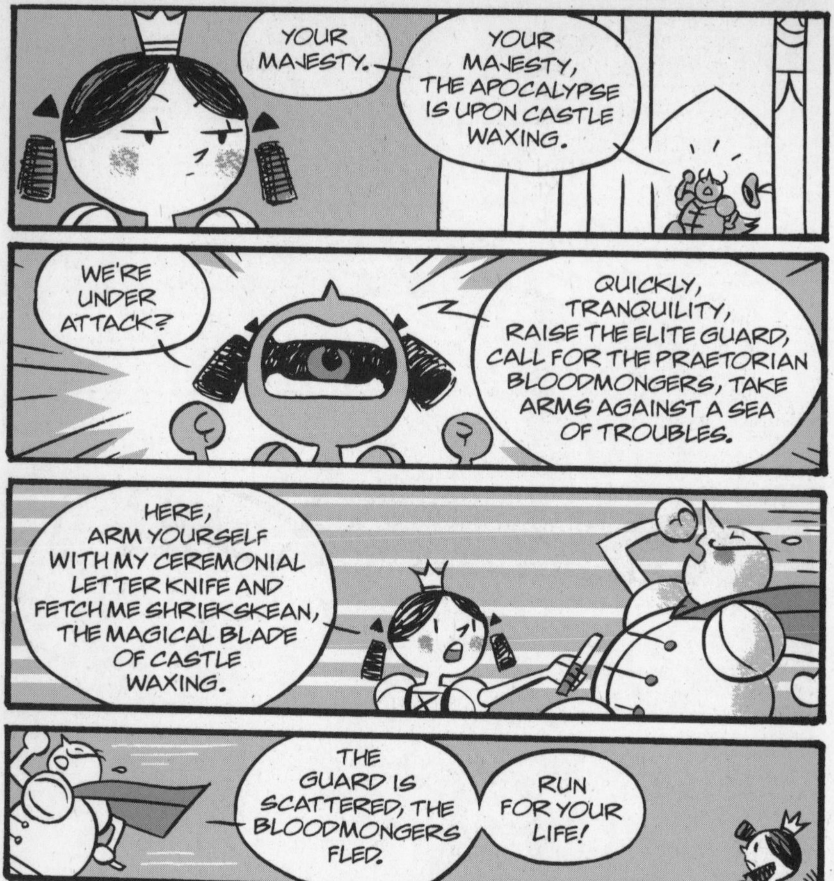
YOUR MAJESTY.
YOUR MAJESTY, THE APOCALYPSE IS UPON CASTLE WAXING.
WE'RE UNDER ATTACK?
QUICKLY, TRANQUILITY, RAISE THE ELITE GUARD, CALL FOR THE PRAETORIAN BLOODMONGERS, TAKE ARMS AGAINST A SEA OF TROUBLES.
HERE, ARM YOURSELF WITH MY CEREMONIAL LETTER KNIFE AND FETCH ME SHRIEKSKEAN, THE MAGICAL BLADE OF CASTLE WAXING.
THE GUARD IS SCATTERED, THE BLOODMONGERS FLED.
RUN FOR YOUR LIFE!

TRANQUILITY'S RAPID FOOTSTEPS ECHOED INTO THE DISTANCE, FOLLOWED BY THE SLAMMING OF THE BACK DOOR. HOLLY WAITED AS THE CACOPHONY OF SCREAMS AND DESTRUCTION GREW CLOSER AND LOUDER.

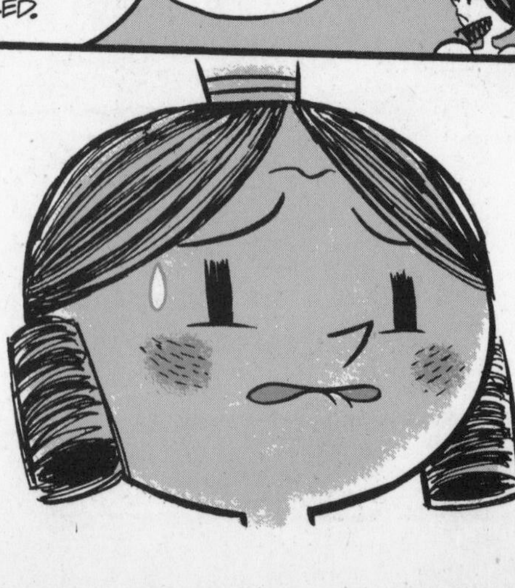

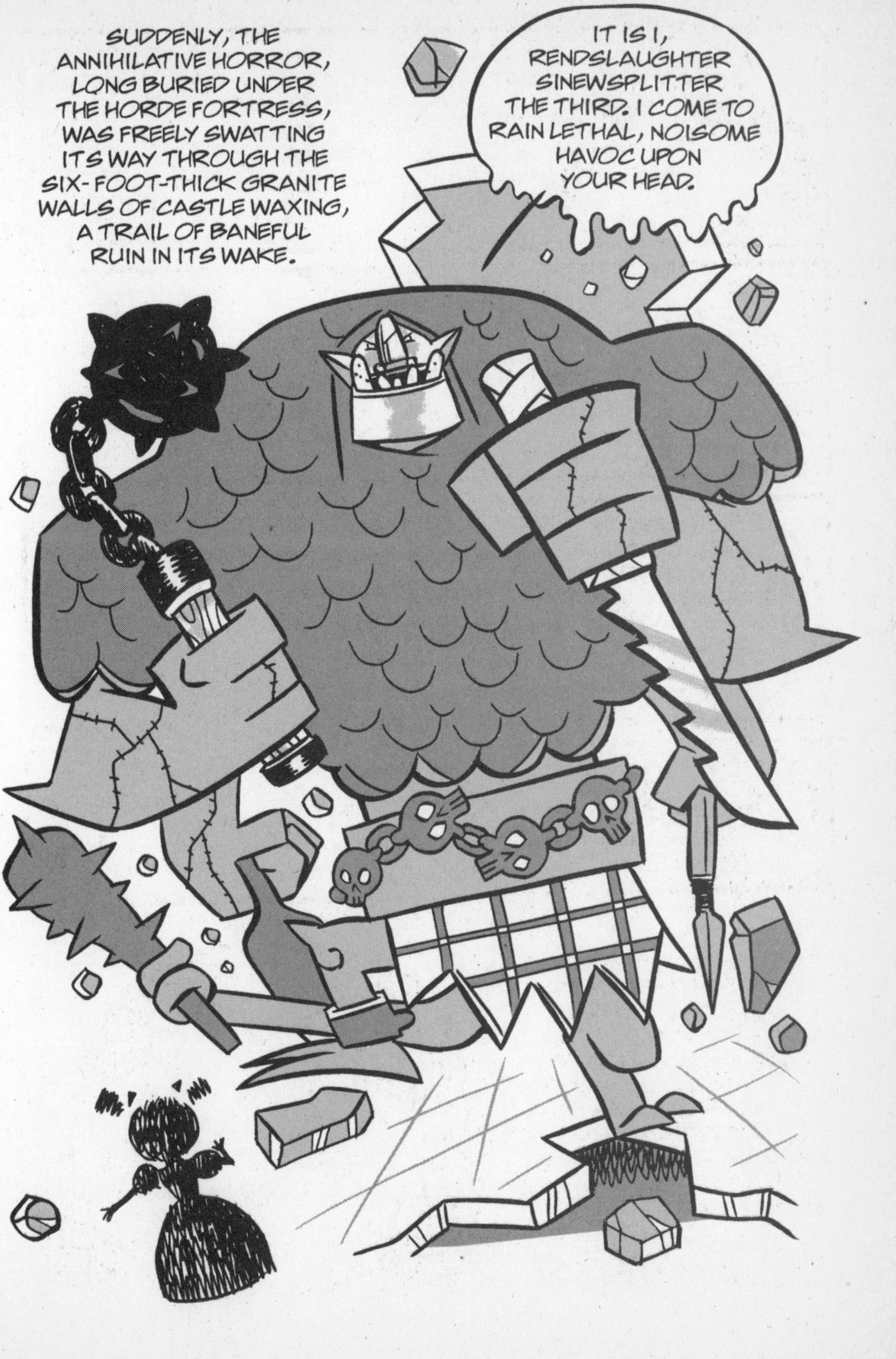
SUDDENLY, THE ANNIHILATIVE HORROR, LONG BURIED UNDER THE HORDE FORTRESS, WAS FREELY SWATTING ITS WAY THROUGH THE SIX-FOOT-THICK GRANITE WALLS OF CASTLE WAXING, A TRAIL OF BANEFUL RUIN IN ITS WAKE.
IT IS I, RENDSLAUGHTER SINEWSPLITTER THE THIRD. I COME TO RAIN LETHAL, NOISOME HAVOC UPON YOUR HEAD.

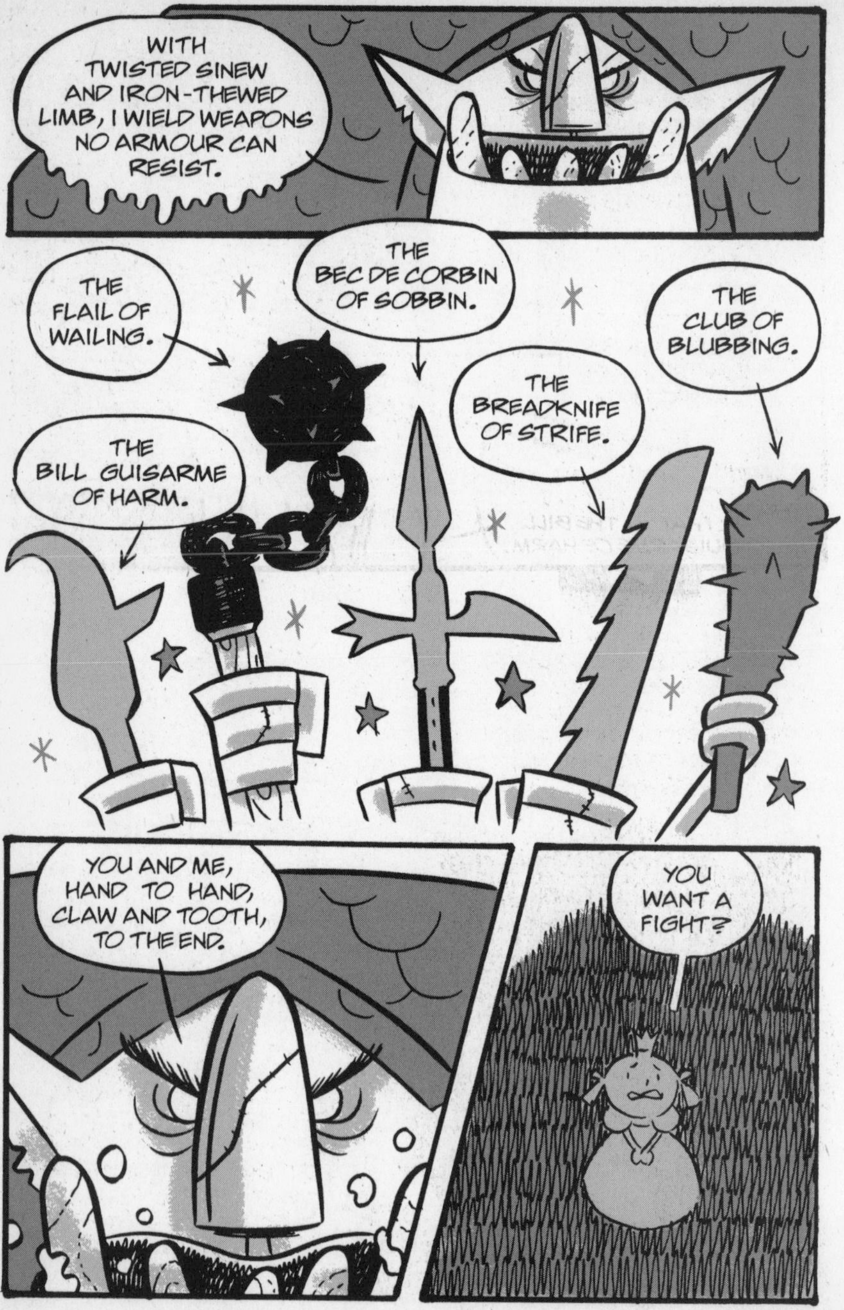
WITH TWISTED SINEW AND IRON-THEWED LIMB, I WIELD WEAPONS NO ARMOUR CAN RESIST.
THE FLAIL OF WAILING.
THE BEC DE CORBIN OF SOBBIN.
THE CLUB OF BLUBBING.
THE BREADKNIFE OF STRIFE.
THE BILL GUISARME OF HARM.
YOU AND ME, HAND TO HAND, CLAW AND TOOTH, TO THE END.
YOU WANT A FIGHT?

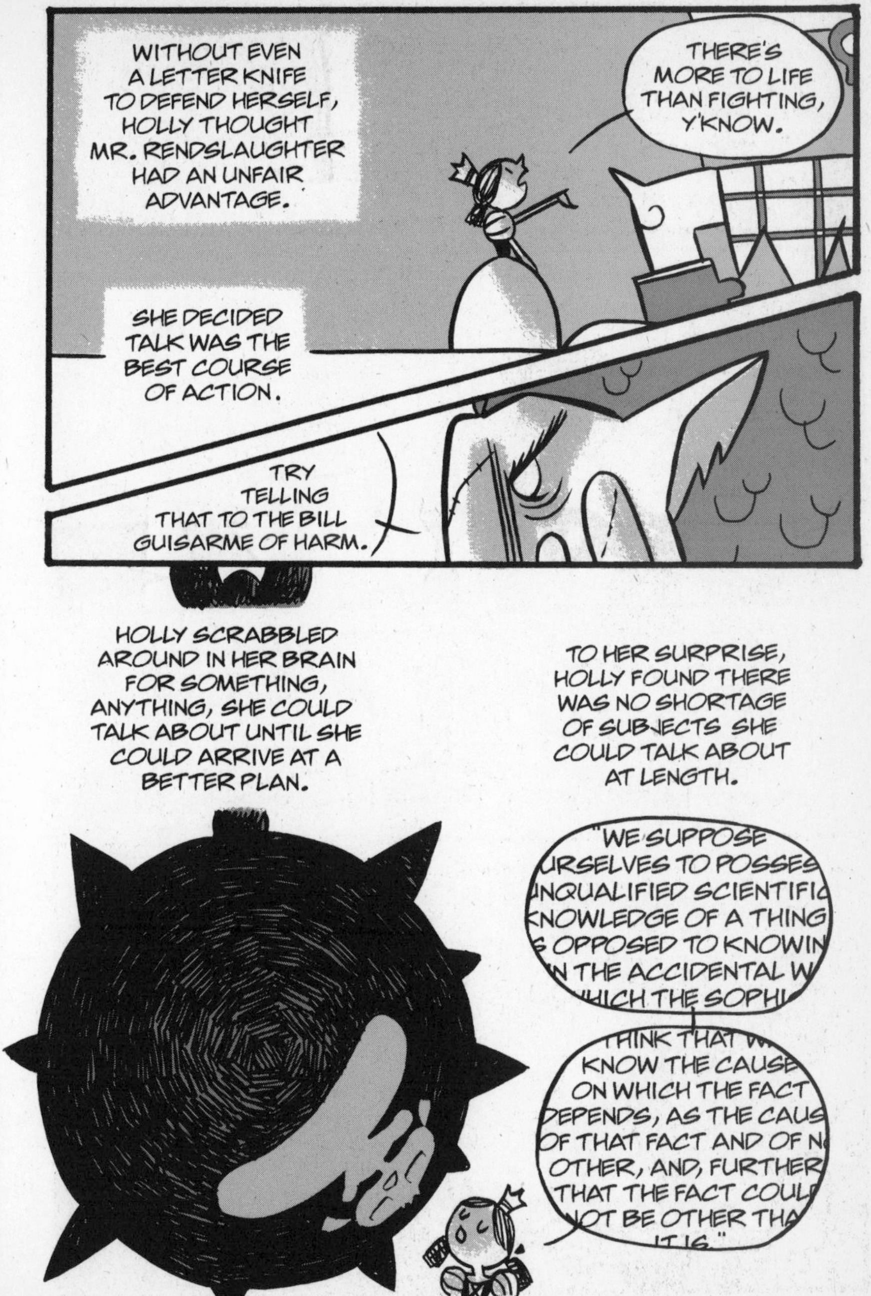
WITHOUT EVEN A LETTER KNIFE TO DEFEND HERSELF, HOLLY THOUGHT MR. RENDSLAUGHTER HAD AN UNFAIR ADVANTAGE.
THERE'S MORE TO LIFE THAN FIGHTING, Y'KNOW.
SHE DECIDED TALK WAS THE BEST COURSE OF ACTION.
TRY TELLING THAT TO THE BILL GUISARME OF HARM.
HOLLY SCRABBLED AROUND IN HER BRAIN FOR SOMETHING, ANYTHING, SHE COULD TALK ABOUT UNTIL SHE COULD ARRIVE AT A BETTER PLAN.
TO HER SURPRISE, HOLLY FOUND THERE WAS NO SHORTAGE OF SUBJECTS SHE COULD TALK ABOUT AT LENGTH.
"WE SUPPOSE URSELVES TO POSSES UNQUALIFIED SCIENTIFIC KNOWLEDGE OF A THING S OPPOSED TO KNOWIN N THE ACCIDENTAL W HICH THE SOPHI
THINK THAT W KNOW THE CAUSE ON WHICH THE FACT DEPENDS, AS THE CAUS OF THAT FACT AND OF N OTHER, AND, FURTHER THAT THE FACT COUL NOT BE OTHER THA IT IS."

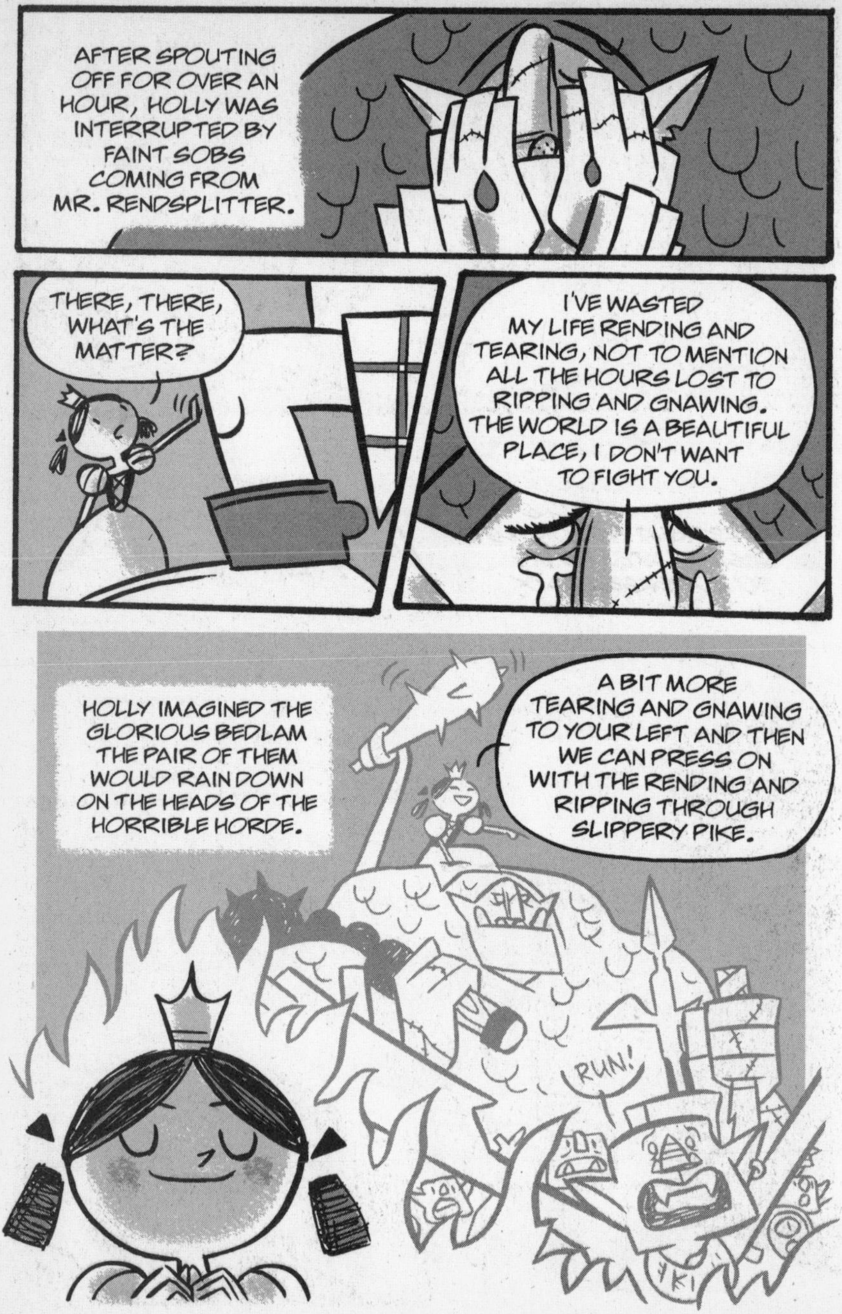
AFTER SPOUTING OFF FOR OVER AN HOUR, HOLLY WAS INTERRUPTED BY FAINT SOBS COMING FROM MR. RENDSPLITTER.
THERE, THERE, WHAT'S THE MATTER?
I'VE WASTED MY LIFE RENDING AND TEARING, NOT TO MENTION ALL THE HOURS LOST TO RIPPING AND GNAWING. THE WORLD IS A BEAUTIFUL PLACE, I DON'T WANT TO FIGHT YOU.
HOLLY IMAGINED THE GLORIOUS BEDLAM THE PAIR OF THEM WOULD RAIN DOWN ON THE HEADS OF THE HORRIBLE HORDE.
A BIT MORE TEARING AND GNAWING TO YOUR LEFT AND THEN WE CAN PRESS ON WITH THE RENDING AND RIPPING THROUGH SLIPPERY PIKE.
RUN!

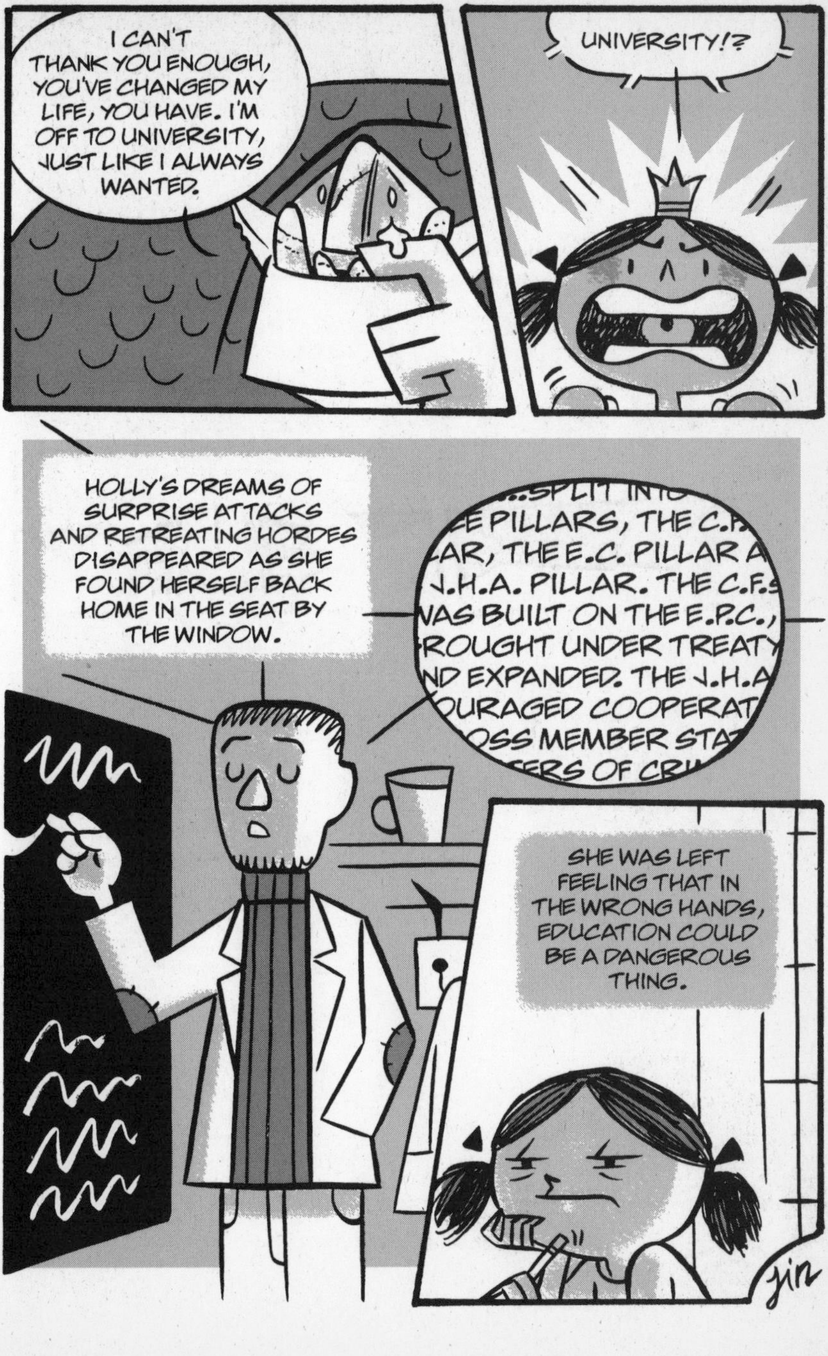
I CAN'T THANK YOU ENOUGH, YOU'VE CHANGED MY LIFE, YOU HAVE. I'M OFF TO UNIVERSITY, JUST LIKE I ALWAYS WANTED.
UNIVERSITY!?
HOLLY'S DREAMS OF SURPRISE ATTACKS AND RETREATING HORDES DISAPPEARED AS SHE FOUND HERSELF BACK HOME IN THE SEAT BY THE WINDOW.
PILLARS, THE C.F.
AR, THE E.C. PILLAR A
J.H.A. PILLAR. THE C.F.
WAS BUILT ON THE E.P.C.,
ROUGHT UNDER TREATY
ND EXPANDED. THE J.H.A
OURAGED COOPERAT
OSS MEMBER STA
SHE WAS LEFT FEELING THAT IN THE WRONG HANDS, EDUCATION COULD BE A DANGEROUS THING.

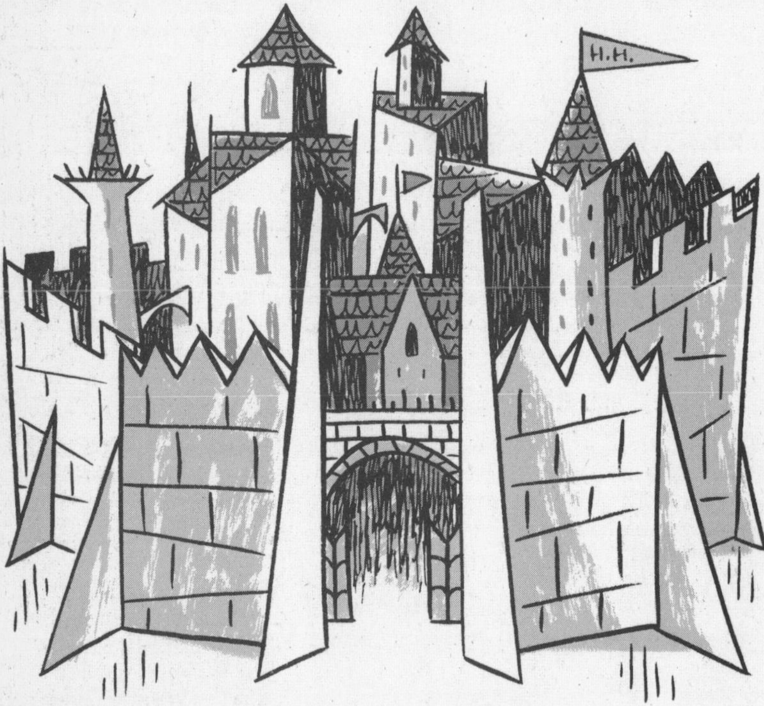
H.H.

www.andiwatson.biz